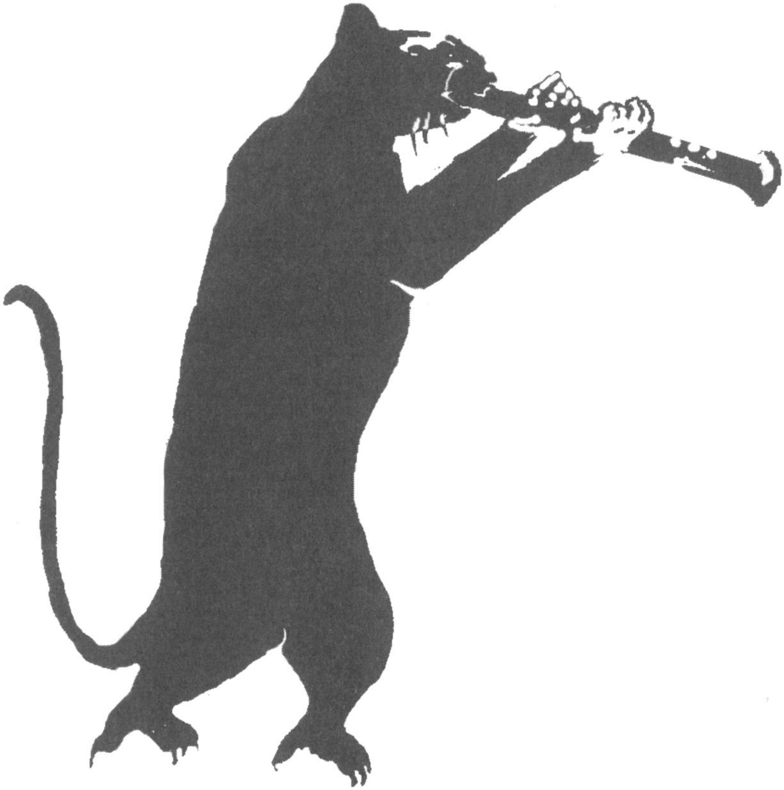

Singer, playwright and award-winning novelist, Mounsi was born in Kabylie, Algeria, and as a child moved to the industrial Parisian suburb Nanterre where this novel is set. His work has been published in the UK in the anthologies *XCiTés: The Flamingo Book of New French Writing* and *Le Foot: The Legends of French Football*. He is the author of four other novels including *The Cities' Ashes*, awarded the Bourse du Centre National du Livre and *Journey of Souls*, winner of the Prix Astrolabe-étonnants voyageurs. *The Demented Dance* received the Prix Malek Haddad-Fondation Nourredine Aba, the Prix France-Maghreb Afrique Méditerranée and the Prix Radio Beur.

THE DEMENTED DANCE

Mounsi

Translated by Lulu Norman

*A life is a book
A book is a life
Mounsi
London 2003*

BlackAmber Books

Published by BlackAmber Books Limited
3 Queen Square
London WCIN 3AU
www.blackamber.com

1 3 5 7 9 10 8 6 4 2

First published in Great Britain by BlackAmber Books 2003

Originally published in French by Editions Stock, Paris
under the title *La Noce des fous*

Copyright © Mounsi 1990
English translation copyright © Lulu Norman 2003

Mounsi asserts the moral right to be identified as the author of this work

This book is supported by the French Ministry for Foreign Affairs, as part of the Burgess Programme headed for the French Embassy in London by the Institut Français du Royaume Uni.

Designed and typeset by James Nunn
Printed in Finland by WS Bookwell

ISBN 1-901969-16-9

Liberté • Égalité • Fraternité
RÉPUBLIQUE FRANÇAISE

All rights reserved. No part of this publication may be reproduced, stored in a retrieval system, or transmitted, in any form or by any means, electronic, mechanical, photocopying, recording or otherwise, without the prior permission of the publishers.

This book is sold subject to the condition that it shall not, by way of trade or otherwise, be lent, re-sold, hired out or otherwise circulated without the publisher's prior consent in any form of binding or cover other than that in which it is published and without a similar condition including this condition being imposed on the subsequent purchaser.

We're like the old new-born
We, the paperback writers

For my son Nassim

For my wife Rabéa

This will remain when I'm no longer young or old
When I have no age

ACKNOWLEDGEMENT

Special thanks to Georgia de Chamberet at BookBlast Ltd writers' agency for making this book happen in the English language.

PROLOGUE

These are lives I ran into inevitably along the way, in every police station which gradually became a familiar habitat. And these words, carved into the benches' blackened wood or on the walls of locked cells with a sharp blade, formed a tapestry before my eyes.

I saw there an unhappy conscience, expressed in the form of a deletion, which is the fate of all writing, when you can only say what life is when you've lost it.

I could have indulged in every debauchery, committed the worst crime, and no one would have been surprised, my victim wouldn't have taken offence. At thirteen, I had pretty much acquired a certain legitimate supremacy. Yet no one would have blinked if I'd taken three bullets in the chest, as if that eventuality would be the crowning glory of my whole life. People only forgive you if they see their own possible story in you. Short of a certain dignity, there's really nothing human left. There've been times I've been lower than a rat. And who wants to see themself like that? Life is for the conquerors and I was conquered. Before I was born. Before life even existed.

On Marguerites inner-city estate in Nanterre, behind a hoarding, I grew up like the bad weed everyone smoked. I learned to fight with the other local boys. Violence was all they had, it was in their guts, bang in the solar plexus, a language of kicks, punches, shouts, screams, and running away, who knows where to. Every one of them was familiar to me. In their faces I sometimes saw an elusive part of myself. I gradually gained a reputation for being a hard case. I scratched a skull on my arm in ink with the nib of the school pen, just to see the fear in people's eyes. They say childhood passes slowly, but mine thrust me into the world of grown-ups. In their eyes I had clear character defects which could only end in crime or failure. Listening to them for too long left me with a feeling of tranquillity and a vague sense of guilt. Little by little, the image I saw reflected in mirrors, as in their eyes, worried me, too. I would just sneak the odd glance. As the years went on, I wasn't sure how to react to the way things were going. And so it went from bad to worse. I can still see those people, teeth clenched in angry impotence, their faces flushed and puffy, greasy noses, big bellies, thin tensed lips quivering with hate, dark eyes looking daggers, stamping their feet, spluttering and yelling: 'You'll come to a bad end, a bad end!'

I hid it but I was getting scared. They seemed so sure of themselves. As if they could fathom the mystery of men and that confusing thing we call life. Even when times were good, I felt obscurely threatened. They didn't know how much they'd scared me, those people, because I'd made fear completely my own. During all my time on this earth their voices have resonated in the background. I could hear their mournful litany and that little sentence, written in a void, would come to my lips: 'You'll come to a bad end.' I held out against them on days I was hungry and cold. Tainted. Filled with shame. But alive, stubbornly alive.

I lived in secret anticipation of this dark premonition, as if the virulence of those words could give birth to the gods and demons that live inside us, and reveal their secrets. The temptation was too great not to find out what they foretold. Did I attempt to expiate my crime by finally committing it? I don't know. But that's how I tried to escape them, to get back to myself.

Incredible as it may seem, as the days passed, I think I accepted their conviction, and even threw myself behind it. The words had been spoken. From first to last, they mattered. As if all my childish terrors had yielded to them. Something happens by chance, God knows why or where it comes from; you're dragged into it and the consequences are extreme. I was what they wanted me to be, and I was it to the bitter end. I had to dredge the depths of my own imagination to save myself from the judgement of others.

Like people driven by raw hunger, who rob graves and feel the skeletons' precious gems rolling beneath their trembling fingers, I took on the power and penalty of sacrilege. My mind racing, hands shaking, by the glow of a lantern, turning over time's remains like forgotten embers in the ashes of a fire, like them I found my life by losing it. Hidden among the dead, crouched behind a gravestone, knife in hand, down alleyways, past epitaphs where the transparent souls of the defunct evaporate from ditches, like them – feverish, frightened by my own daring, hair wet, shirt stuck to the skin – the same night awoke in me a lugubrious feeling of intimacy.

There's a split second in life, the consequences of which will be felt throughout our existence. A mysterious action dominates it, an impulse that changes its course and closes to us the peaceful path of honest men, leading us to fulfil the curse, tainted by the stain of blood. I was never sure I existed. I was always confused by a vague recollection of having seemed to live. I resided inside life as if it were some squalid story, witness to a murder in which I was both the killer and the corpse. I still flinch from what I saw in everyone's eyes, from executioner to victim. There's a secret madness in us that we perpetrate without even realising, a sudden intuition of our souls that lies beyond all logic, a gesture with a meaning that eludes our conscience, a movement of the body that happens outside us and far outstrips the mind. Everything vibrates through the nerves, unto infinity, in the enactment of this esoteric tragedy, of which we only glimpse the occasional manifestation: it's the lonely course of a power that overtakes us. In the uncertain tension of the melting world, something is played out around us, in the hidden cavities of stones, in the veins of wood, which sets fire to the walls and roofs. An imperceptible vibration in the still of the afternoon.

A thousand unknown things rise from the depths of the earth and pass through us in a flash of lightning, warping our bodies and our minds. Some men's destinies are linked to disaster, to which they climb as to a peak of perfection. The bitter desire to live one's death so as to be reborn is a different power. Propelled by our bodies, there are acts we cannot comprehend. We commit them. Their meaning only becomes clear much later on in time, little by little, and sometimes never. My wrists handcuffed, as if on the path of ancient trails, unhurried, I followed that prophecy to the end, where everything begins. When the prison warder opened the cell door, I had a feeling of déjà vu, as if nothing happens that hasn't already been lived, repeated to the point where you might easily say to yourself, 'Hang on, the chair that was here before has gone.' I think I felt that kind of detachment from life from the very beginning. That confusion may have prefigured another kind of guilt, transcending the world of men.

It wasn't within the jurisdiction of the police or the law courts, but I couldn't agree to being a victim, in other words an innocent declared guilty. Something deep inside me wanted to deserve my punishment. When my father came to register my birth, the town hall official forgot to write down the day, month and year I was born. The yellowed form still states 'probable d.o.b –'. I'm afraid that since then, all the incidents or events that occurred with the passage of time – past, present or to come – have been nothing but dreams. I've had a kind of relentless hesitancy about myself, an extreme doubt that made me ask myself, when I saw my reflection in the mirror, if I wasn't just an optical illusion. Can you assure me that such a person, who looks like me, ever existed?

The age-old, the same, eternal, heaving, blackened suburbs that surrounded the Red belt of working-class neighbourhoods, and all that went before. Housing estates as far as the eye could see, thrown up on waterlogged ground, in a landscape of factory chimneys which spread noxious fumes around them, so that in winter the snow itself would fall from a sky stained with soot. The whole area was covered in a piss-yellow rusty crust. Mud, rain, coal dust, splashes of tar, trees stunted at ground level. The high wind lifted swirling clouds of rubbish that lay rotting beside the lead, chipboard and breezeblock maisonettes. Then you would see the silhouettes of the poor, fleeing under sheets of rain, or gangs of kids wandering unpaved paths, looking for a bit of bread or rummaging through the bins. But that's all forgotten now, as are the prowlers of times gone by.

Today, the red-brick blocks of flats are home to a throng of immigrants, come from the four corners of the earth to seek a haven of hope. The yells and shrieks of their children at play rise up from below the ring road. Most of the foreigners who settle here eventually put down roots. They work hard to feed their families. Across the low skies, trails of smoke gather into thick, greyish waves and fill the air, pulled this way and that by the wind. Down there, at the fringes of the dry land and desolate landscape, on these far-flung, naked confines where life is so vulnerable, it's impossible to harbour any illusions about a harmonious outcome in the hereafter.

This is neither heaven nor hell. It's the world of men. A matter of fact. Here we are. This is my inner city. Far removed from the Greek city, the horses and chariots, and the earth which gave rise to gods among half-broken columns that still retain the beauty of immortal ruins. Where I live, the entrance to hell lies on the west side of the sinuous, rapid course of the capital's ring road. Towards the alley that circles the rough façades, at the threshold of a world where only dreams are real and life does not exist. In this scrapheap of modern buildings, higher than the pylons planted in the black mud, walls grow like prisons, supported by thin partitions. The inhabitants are only distinguishable by their accents. Birds fly through the poisoned air. In that leaning, twisted tower block, behind the windows, where the washing is hung out, blackened with soot before it's dry, that's where my mother shat me. In one of those model dormitories stacked on top of each other like coffins where no dead man of antiquity ever lay. Bloody birth. She died. Her form flew away. Lyrebird or phoenix? Who cares? Her face is buried in the soil of my birth, that pit which is the impoverished homeland of the dead.

Through the partitions, as through a half-open window, come the sounds of TVs, quarrelling neighbours, screams, curses and threats, and the radio bawling the same old songs. Beds creak and doors slam. Lives are parked here like the shells of cars in a big cement car park. Each in its place. Immobile. As the years go on, the sweat of exhausted men and harassed women seeps into the dilapidated walls, into the blue overalls and the lining of clothes. In the bathrooms, the girls' perfumes and stale beauty creams mingle with the smell of mouldy wallpaper. Kitchen fumes and a nauseating stench rise from the rusty pipes, a lingering odour of dungeons. It's like the breath of death, a foul smell in the mouth and the air, a build-up of decay, a pitiless stink that inflames the sinuses. There are those who die, unsure they've ever lived, while others go on living, trapped in a habit they cannot break. Scorned faces swarm in the obscure light. A thousand lives, all the same, today and yesterday. A mass of humanity, humiliated, trampled, crushed, spreading across the earth like sediment.

Here, people wait. That's all they do. They've stopped at the edge of themselves. They emerge for a second, as though something might happen, then they shrink back. Blood flows, shapeless water, in their veins. They live like fish that still remember the sea and knock against the glass sides of aquariums, turning back on themselves. They enter and leave life bearing its secrets of sadness. In the streets, past dead ends, their ghosts are swept off by the wind that carries everything away. I see the cortège go by. I call out. I wave but they pass by. They can't hear me now. They're too far away, braced against the night like peasants labouring in a field. Yet I knew them well. Every old man, every child, every family, I know by sight. Like defeated soldiers, they've retreated. On their faces, the mask of centuries. The entire foreign legion of solitude – Italian, Chinese, French, Turks, Cossacks, and the rest – conquerors of the new world, whose voices blend with the language of the shades. They are far gone in forgetting. I've seen whole families, generations, pass by, squeezed together, slipping between the muddy earth and the evening's still-pink sky. Their resigned shadows have faded into the night. All my people who have left this life disappeared there, the same way everything will be lost.

We were an imaginary demarcation line, an equator on the world's circumference. From time to time, geographers would speak of us in high-up places, but in reality they forgot us, like sailors lost on the open sea. Our boats slowly rotted in their memories. Occasionally, alone, men would come, faces draped in white, hiding their hatred in the uniform hood; their eyes gleamed like rats' eyes. They were nostalgic for the barracks, for the days when the wind from the Aurès made the blue, white and red flags flap at the summit of the Djurdjura mountains. The blind fury that drove them was the kind that nothing can quell. The heavy clang of their iron boots rang in our heads.

What's the point of begging for mercy from a pathetic heaven that has no pity for anyone? I've lived here alongside so many others about whom I remember and know nothing any longer. Pale, feverish people, twisted on an ancient grief. Solitary men, their faces in their fists, rejected by other men. The mass of their corpses fills the void. They've flown away over black roofs, beyond the city walls. They floated off in the wind that pushed them from left to right, but kept on going through the clouds. I saw them turn into little dots in the sky and then be extinguished among the stars. Their sign had already been hammered out in other constellations, an outline of men between earth and sky, where destinies are written.

There is nothing else on earth. Nothing. And no one. With our eyes trained on the shifting horizon of time, life will pass over us and through us like wind. From dawn till night, we'll be there, far from you, at the furthest reach of solitude, in that land of men without race or name, shaded by the walls of that city of metal and cement where it all began.

It's impossible to go back. The road has crumbled behind us. It's so far away now. The tarmac has caved in and collapsed into the ravine. There is nothing left in the world; everything has been swallowed up. We will never retrace our steps. We have left the roads, the trees, the houses and the years behind us.

Yet, in the enigma of things, we too were children once. Saints, angels and virgins are made of plaster. But we are flesh and blood, bone and sex. Beneath the whitewash, what's left of the statues? Unsettling dawns may break and the hour chime in cathedrals . . . *Sonnez les matines, sonnez les matines*, ding dong damned, ding dong damned. The castles of our childhood are buried under the sand, beyond a dead sea, in the broken blue.

Fania 'the rose', I see her now the way she first appeared to me, reapplying her make-up with the earnest gestures of a little girl, black on her lashes and red on her lips. She shone with whatever it is that misfortune adds to beauty. Something so tender it hurt me to look at her. Her madonna's face conjured the winter light that filters through the stained glass in cathedrals, an indescribable radiance. She bore that strange pious sorrow which emanates from the velvety softness of frescoes.

I was struck by her paleness. She was wearing a plain,

austere white dress. Her long hair tumbled down her back. A little gold cross adorned her neck and her slender shoulders jutted out at angles. She wore no bracelet or ring. Her china-blue eyes were like two little lakes of tears. It was odd, that impression of childish gravity in her eyes. She was barely sixteen but life had already marked her. She had also opened her eyes too soon. You could see she had lost her illusions before she'd even begun to menstruate. Girls who open their legs too early have something in their eyes that lingers, a sadness, a wound to the iris. Like those dolls you wake up and put to bed. It is just the same. Suffering is as old as time, it's ancient, much older than wrinkles. Like ivy, it dies where it clings. As a little girl, in her flowery dress, Fania would go begging up in the rich part of town with her young gypsy mother, who nursed another child fastened on her breast. They knew all the roads that led up to the grand avenues, to the thresholds of the department stores with their luxurious window displays. Sitting on the ground, hands outstretched, they'd catch the legs of the passers-by. Her mum hid her face under an old headscarf. So many people, so many feet passing level with her forehead, their steps sending out vibrations. At night, exhausted, they'd slowly make their way back to the metal caravan parked along the pavement at Porte de Montreuil. She stopped begging when she got too old for it and left her clan.

Fania joined those gangs of kids who spend their lives waiting anxiously for morning, hiding behind their sunglasses as if their blind eyes were dissolving in the sun. Sometimes, some of them walk through the seedy side of town, looking for a needle with no thread to sew up the ever-widening holes in their veins. They migrate to the basement dealers.

In Strasbourg-Saint-Denis metro station, a quick brush against the wall where three or four Africans are arguing. In the palms of their hands, little five-gram packets still glisten with saliva. A glance, a nod, a wink, a secret sign, and the kids get on the train, headed for the agreed destination further down the line. There the dealer goes to fetch the little packets hidden under the ballast between the rails. He steps down on the track and crosses over, defying the electric current and its eight hundred volts. He makes the delivery as arranged, then returns to base on the metro platform. Here, and elsewhere, dealers favour cutting their drugs with rat poison, plaster, strychnine or laxative. These kids with watery sky-blue eyes can barely remember who they are. They got lost in some sordid old piss-hole of a bar, a hangout for police informers, in hock to heroin and the drug squad. Hunched over, they shuffle off, coughing and spitting, heads lolling slightly, as if the gusts of wind would blow them this way and that or carry them off because of their bird-like weight.

All that's left of the fleeting purity of the snowy mornings of childhood, before the dirt of the days descends, is the sky, measured out in the dropper of the syringe that shoots up the ultimate fix. And the ache of need that digs a hole in their bellies.

Oh Fania. I remember the day I clung on to her wrist, to keep hold of whatever it is that outlives the body. All that remains is the smell of burnt grass. The sky is bare and empty. Here and beyond, lives are swept off in a dusty wind, a wind that burns and bleaches everything: faces, bones, stones, earth and the charred leaves of the tree.

In the middle of the capital's ring road, between the lanes, surrounded by the rumble of metal and the rush of cars, motorbikes, buses, the stink of petrol and gas and the deafening city roar, a man prays. He has spread out a white cloth before him and neither the curses nor the jeers of the drivers interrupt his slow prostration. He prays on the tarmac as if on holy ground. Slowly, he bows his coppery face. In the middle of the ring road, he's heard the muezzin's call to evening prayer, a voice borne by the wind like a lament for his heart to hear. All around him he feels the breath of silence. As if the world had stopped moving and speaking. As if the cars had turned to stone. Mouth to the ground, he breathes deeply, listening to the blood throbbing in his throat and his ears. His cheekbones jut out from a dark, bearded face; he wears an old cap on his head, askew, and his eyes are glazed over. His shirt and trousers hang pitifully from his frame. His hands are sticky with a blackish grease. He throws back his head and begins to pray. He leans forward through the looking-glass, towards the palms of his hands. He stays bent over like this for a long time. His gaze lies elsewhere, beyond the world of men and city walls. He stares into the distance, far away, to the deepest recess of the sky, where lies infinity. In the sunlight he sees white cities, springs, caravans of camels and donkeys loaded with provisions. In the middle of the ring road floats the mirage of a minaret. In his eyes: hunger, thirst, exhaustion, madness. He prays on the tarmac as if on holy ground.

Up a sandy path, he follows the blackened riverbed of dried-up torrents, he walks under a sky of light. He inhales the breath of the wind. He goes down to a spring where he bathes his face between his hands, kneeling on the soil like a man returned from a long journey. So he remains, on the cracked, hardened, baked earth. The sun at its zenith burns like a flame. He is over there now, in the midst of songs, locusts, wasps, among the shepherds and the herds of goats and sheep and clumps of nettles. Over there, amid the clear, echoing voices of women with long, henna-stained fingers, singing softly, cradling infants in their arms, lazily batting off midges that dance and buzz over their heads. He recognises the parchment faces of old men and women who lean back on walls of dry stone and mud. He remembers their first names.

He forgets the concrete walls between which I would wait for him, eyes straining, as if, every time I heard the door bang, it would open to reveal the light of his smile, a ray of sunlight through the bars.

Piled in the kitchen or hidden under the bed were his bottles of plonk. Each drop of shame drained to the dregs, like some poisonous wine, so that even gushing fountains of fresh water would seem bitter to his thirst. I could see him drinking straight from the bottle. Where else could he have filled up and emptied himself of so much at the same time? Gradually he spoke to no one, not even me. He made noises, gurgles. That was it.

In the roar of the traffic, four men in white coats alighted from a vehicle with a red cross on the side. They lifted him by the hands and legs, launching him into the air. He wound up on the hood of the ambulance with his arms outstretched in the shape of a cross. Spread-eagled, he groaned weakly and closed his eyes.

'He's blind drunk,' said the driver.

'I saw God!' the man screamed.

The four uniformed nurses from the local hospital had to use a straitjacket. They whisked him away with the siren wailing. Next morning I was woken by banging on the door. The doorbell was broken. I got up to answer, half dressed. Everyone was there, a whole herd of them in the room. First, the neighbour and the social worker, then the concierge with men from the Department of Health. The place had a musty smell, a stench of wine and a faint odour of tobacco.

'Unbelievable. Got to like filth to live in this dump,' the concierge kept repeating as she opened the cupboards.

Someone remembered you shouldn't talk like that in front of 'the kid'.

'Ha! Don't you think I'm saying it for his benefit?'

The man from the council responsible for our block put his hand on my shoulder in a friendly gesture and assured me, ruffling my hair affectionately, that he'd called social services so I'd have everything I needed.

'It's for your own good,' he added.

As if I cared, about my good or anything else. I wasn't even listening to them. I couldn't even cry. I felt like a dried-up fountain. For years he'd worked in one of those factories where a greasy chain clanks over the workers' heads. In time with the rhythm of the machine, the men's fingers fitted metal parts. He laboured twelve hours a day, between the double row of machine tools where each man had his own bench, two teams operating in shifts, each of their movements minutely calculated and sequenced beforehand.

At the end of the day he would come home. Drained.

Every morning he'd set off again. One day the factory shut down. He was laid off. But the chain went on revolving in his worn-out brain. I think part of him got caught in the grinding wheel. Little by little he drifted into a kind of stupor. Stopping in the street he'd mutter aloud prayers in Arabic that I didn't understand. His fingers edged along old prayer beads, absent-mindedly, as if he were already dead.

I don't think my father really was mad. He was just afraid of his own shadow. Times were hard: bailiffs, repossessions, due dates, threats of eviction for non-payment of rent. When they came, those law enforcers and council bureaucrats, I could hear them laughing under their breath at my father's accent.

'Got enough money to drink, though, eh, Mustapha...?'

The entire fate of mankind and of the world lay in that remark, in that wickedness which is everywhere. Ever since people have suffered, they would have known if a little love existed somewhere, here, there, on earth or in heaven.

With his pitiful blind man's shuffle, he would slowly make his way back from the bars, his head lolling. He walked the narrow city streets later and later into the night. Faces would appear in the windows, people would point at him and laugh. I heard his heavy steps echoing in the stairwell. More than once he'd trip on a step or hurt his head on the corridor wall. Forehead pressed against the door, he'd try to fit the tip of his key in the keyhole. Not finding the light switch he'd let a match singe his skin as it burnt out. I'd get up to open the door. He'd be standing there asleep on his feet. I could smell the cheap wine on his drunken body. At home I'd sometimes hide the bottles. He'd hunt for them as a thirsty man hunts for a bubbling spring.

In my eyes' unswerving gaze I hold on to the saddest early memory of them all, that which I discerned in his illiterate eyes as he shuffled towards his damnation, incapable of perceiving those around him. He would drift into a strange sleep disturbed by trances, sudden jerks and flashes of delirium. Lying in the same bed, I'd hold him in my arms to protect him from the rats and snakes and all the wild animals that slept by his bedside. I was haunted by his face. I watched him sleep, the way he would do one day, for ever, eyelids closed once and for all.

Feverish, wild-eyed, he'd jolt awake, his throat dry, dripping with sweat, lips trembling. He'd try to stop gasping and catch his breath. I would turn on the light and show him the animals that fled for cover, crawling and slithering across the floor. Pacified, he'd smile at me by way of apology for waking me in the middle of the night. I knew that at the next bout of drinking, the moment he had nodded off, the rats lurking in the holes in the walls would return to make his teeth chatter with horror. He shivered and I waited for dawn. Outside, the bustle of life began in absolute indifference. Those who have experienced nights like these no longer have any liking for sleep. He was so harmless, so vulnerable.

Later, with all the paltry ferocity I could muster, I avenged him with love and a hatred of the world. I wreaked my revenge on everything that crossed my path: man, woman or beast. There is no remorse in my soul for what I did. No one is innocent. No one. Not them, nor I, nor you. I have long felt the urge to disfigure, to defile every living creature, by branding them with the stamp of my life. It is fascinating, other people's suffering, their ability to express terror. Those screams, like a cry outside yourself, uttered by someone else, but in which you hear your own voice. Curiously, later, as I went on my way, I'd often run into tramps with shabby clothes and dishevelled hair and the crazed look of a prophet. Those men who stagger along the pavements, they'd grab my sleeve as I passed and stare at me for ages, motionless. In their gaze I would see my father's eyes. Panicked and afraid, I'd back away.

In our deserted home, I leaned over to pick up the pieces of broken bottles scattered on the ground with the earnest, silent concentration of a child gathering autumn leaves. All I had left of my father was what memory offered, until I forgot everything. From care centres, to foster families, to hostels.

On days mild like sweet cherubim, I'd stand, legs apart, knees slightly bent, back arched and piss through the air towards the sky. Perhaps I was already pissing at God. Gradually, I learned not to fear anything any longer, but just to let things take their course and wait for the inevitable outcome. During the day, I'd never tire of staring at the sky. And at night, the dormitory ceilings. I pressed down my fingers on my eyes as hard as I could, so I'd see stars. In the morning my eyelids were black and blue. I wondered if that was how you looked when you died.

As for my father, I saw him only once more, by chance, in the street. But I made sure he didn't see me. Although his hair had gone white and his back was hunched, I recognised him by his brown-eyed gaze, intensified by his emaciated body.

On Saturday night, the men come down from beneath the capital's ring roads, heading for the junction where the avenues meet. Like a river estuary entering the sea, they flow towards the city where the lights flash and dazzle their eyes. With radios blaring, singing at the tops of their voices, down they flood in waves, drifting along to be swallowed up in the eddying swirl of the pavements. They get drunk at bar counters. They roam all those streets where the crowd heaves and jostles, constantly ducking in and out of the sex shops and bars, while the cars pile down avenues that seem to go on for ever. It's night-time, the city lights up, headlights sweep the streets with brushes of light. Car lights shine, noises reverberate, tipsy passers-by fall over, pick themselves up and dodge between the lines of stationary traffic.

Blurry-eyed tramps amble by, with a thirst on them that nothing can quench; backs bent, a vacant gaze, their threadbare coats patched and torn again by nights spent sleeping on the ground or in doorways. Soldiers out on a bender and jeering sailors with beery breath soliloquise under red, green, orange neon signs and hazy lights. They disappear into the churning crowd, the rumble of cars and the intoxicating smell of burning petrol that makes the head ache.

All these people come and go, walk and run. Their shadows overlap, their clothes crease and give off static as they push past. The street lights flash on and off, reflected in shop windows. Lights blink orange, mauve, purple. Under the moon, the stars glitter, traffic lights beam red, amber, green, orange indicators, honking horns. Engines rev, tyres squeal, brakes screech. A group of men has stopped on the pavement, standing quite still and staring at the entrance to a building. They puff on cigarettes, sending blue spirals of smoke into the night. Behind a tiny glass door, ajar onto a long, narrow corridor, a half-naked woman waits for morning. All through the night she's been shoved backwards onto an old, stained mattress and possessed for a few seconds by ghosts which vanish into the air. The house has tall, barred windows. In the milky light of the porch, through the bars, you can see women young and old, so sad it hurts to look at them. Zohra from Oran was among them. Her dazzling smile flashed gold teeth. We were afraid of her, Bako and I, because she had the power to cast spells.

In the city centre, behind the vast glass restaurant windows, waiters appear dressed in white, pushing small trolleys laden with dishes of all colours. Round tables draped in snowy tablecloths, bunches of flowers in crystal vases and silver domes. Perfumed women, men wearing suits and white scarves go in, pushing the revolving door. Noses pressed to the glass, we could see them, those gorgeous ladies, sitting around artfully arranged dishes, dabbing their pretty lips with damask napkins. We were already fantasising about them.

In the streets people hurry by, their arms full of presents and provisions. In the pale light of the street lamps, by the buildings where the roads are quiet and the houses locked up, we walked along as if we were alone in the world.

Winter was harsh. The pavements were covered by a thin layer of frost, the soles of our shoes gaped and let in the wind. Because we roamed the streets, we only ever washed in the rain. We'd hang out, free to wander, a law unto ourselves, our existence an aimless drifting. We lived impulsively. What I remember of those days is the smell of a candle burnt till dawn. Life is always a little further on, its borders as yet unknown. We had nothing to lose but the skin on our bones. Nothing.

Along a tight, dark alley that climbed to the heights of the city, Bako and I waited, hidden in a doorway, one hungry day spent begging the price of a dream. We were there in the night. Sounds of laughter and Christmas carols, the mournful voices of cathedral choirs reached us, echoing strangely in the solitude of the street. 'Silent night, holy night, all is calm, all is bright.' Bako was moved, enthralled by this music. He was probably remembering Christmas mornings as a child with his parents, opening presents under the tree glittering with tinsel. Although he was frozen stiff, his fingers still clutched his flick-knife, even as he rubbed his hands together for warmth. He had the innate gift of being able to play with his blade like the bow of a violin. The passage was so narrow, the man or woman we were waiting for didn't stand a chance. The stink from the dustbins filled my nostrils, reminding me yet again of life's close connection to decay. Around us everything was still.

Alert, we waited till our eyes became accustomed to the dark. With a trembling hand, Bako signalled that a man was coming. I had a thin, flexible blade more than fifteen centimetres long hidden in the lining of my jacket. Bako flicked open his knife. Silently, he adjusted it a notch, and gripped it in a hand that had steadied. I could see the man at the end of the street in the orangey streetlight, just opposite. Our hearts pounded in time with our breathing, which got faster the closer he came. First we heard the dull thud of his feet then, more distinctly, each step followed by a silent pause before the next. I estimated the distance he had left. He'd just crossed the last metre that lay between us. I could already feel his breath, so close it filled the confines of the alley. Soon he was within range. I stepped out, staring at him hard.

'What do you want from me?' he asked, turning his stooped body.

'Your wallet! Shift your arse or we'll cut you,' Bako shouted, his voice muffled and menacing. The blue steel blade in his raised hand sliced the air, clasped between thumb and index finger. The man took a step forward but stopped and stared at us.

'Here,' he said and threw his wallet at our feet. He shook his head and blinked, with a pitying air. He looked at us in silence, as if he couldn't believe his eyes. We stood there, caught in the neon light. We fled, slithering along the wall. Further on, sitting on the ground, hair stuck to our cheeks with sweat, we slowly swelled our lungs to inhale the fumes from a bag of glue.

I'd just had a terrible experience, that of fear, a kind of physical spasm. It was no good taking deep breaths, nothing could stop my thumping heart. It had never before occurred to us to be dishonest in any way. We had to grab the least flicker of human life on offer, whatever the risks. We were drawn to it by the very nature of the life we had been leading.

I was always the class dunce in the few lessons I attended, which made me a target for teasing. But you get used to not shining in life, like those urchins immersed in the cold filth of baptismal fonts who wander naked through the streets, driven by pain. Poverty has no need of embellishment – that is its badge of glory. It raises its young with all the strength it can muster.

Thrown out of ten schools, I'd become an animal on the run. When I turned round to write on the blackboard, white chalk in hand, a big hole showed in my raggedy clothes. My humiliation made the boys' eyes light up with malicious joy. My clothes were dirty. In front of all those rich kids, I felt worthless. I dreamed of derailing all their trains so they'd never arrive at the station. I'd spit in the inkwells and drop my teachers' chalk in them to soak. Whatever I did, I ended up twisted. Even my handwriting sloped to the left and then to the right. It wasn't round or sharp, just disjointed and shapeless.

I was only happy in year 1 of secondary school, in Mademoiselle Karina's class. All I learned there was to smell the wafting mists of her perfume and take in the swish of her lacy petticoats. My eyes sought out the openings of her low-necked blouses; a hint of cherry floated there. She would always walk up and down the rows of tables like the movement of the tides. An erotic ebb and flow, frozen in time. The click of her stiletto heels echoed in my maddened brain. She had the troubling, voluptuous beauty of women in tales of old, the disturbing femininity of an Amazon. She couldn't help but reveal the splendour of her charms. I'd have liked to rest my young head in the cleavage between her massive breasts, explore the long curves of her magnificent body. Her contours seemed to call out for and deserve immense love. What wouldn't I have given to be the one to take her and arouse her! I'd recognise the essence of her own secret smell from all the rest. It was a headiness unlike any other, a scent that clings to the nostrils.

Sometimes she'd dictate the précis of a book, perched on the edge of my table, planted right in front of me, outlined against the paling light coming through the windows. She seemed to take pleasure in her strange silhouette and stature that towered over me, displaying her intimate difference. In the middle of a paragraph, with a swivel of her head, her green eyes would suddenly rest on me. I felt my trousers tighten. A faint smile played across her face. Bending gracefully over my exercise book, her chest passed over my eyes like night over day. Her soft voice would say: 'Try to concentrate on your spelling, Tarik.' A mad urge came over me to kiss her opulent breasts with their milky fragrance, lolling in front of my mouth like fruit on a tree. Her left breast in particular seemed huge, bigger than her right, or maybe that was just because of the beating of her heart. I could see the thin strap of her bra over the fragile hollow of her shoulder, under her silk blouse.

When I went too far, disrupting the class with my bravado, Mademoiselle Karina would make me go under her desk to calm down. What delicious punishment! While she corrected our exercise books, I could make out the soft hair of her golden fleece, satin-smooth, and the three white fleur-de-lis embroidered on her knickers. I could have spent my entire life between her thighs, which she'd cross and uncross, with a slight rasp of her stockings, trying to get comfortable. What did I care for comfort? What a way to go, released in the supreme moment beneath delicate, transparent lingerie, amid the provocative armour of girdles, bras, suspender belts, hoisted like frigates' sails into pure, exposed matter. Deep in the aroma of voluptuous flesh, in among the downy strands of hair, you'd leave as you'd come, craving an infinite caress, a final farewell to sorrow, delicately, in full poetic flight, with a thousand whispered sweet nothings. At that age, all you see of love is its rose-tinted aspect. Just one little controlled, discreet, elegant orgasm.

Under her desk, in the intimacy of her underwear, between her legs, precisely where the elastic of the suspenders garrotted the skin of her thighs, my mind concentrated on her pussy, I breathed into her curls. Your mind inside someone's knickers, that's rare, but it's amazing. I was there, I can vouch for it. I was carried off in a dream. I inhaled deeply. My nose reached into the origin of life. I hallucinated curls of fur. That was my whole life, right there. I've always preferred the all-seeing eyes of voyeurs to the predictions of clairvoyants. Such humility comes from my childhood. I was born for keyholes, needles' eyes, for captivating little things like Mademoiselle Karina's lace flounces that hid her little hole at the depths of the sea. She liked beautiful things, no nylon or jersey knit for her. The outline of her little magical slit slept in a customised silk casket, palpitating softly like a fledgling's heart. Under the fabric of her dress, I could breathe it in like the perfume of a flower; her scent spread inside me.

My obsessive love had driven me to steal the pair of stockings from the drawer in her desk. In the evening, back at the home, I would double-lock the door and measure the length of her legs with my long ruler. I'd go right up to the top. I measured each centimetre of my desire. At night, I'd put them between my thin thighs. I'd go to bed, the better to dream about her. I'd pull my cock like elastic. Oh, how I wrung dreams from it with my left hand and my right, but the sap wouldn't come.

I was sad, I couldn't sleep any more, so I'd get up. In front of the mirror, I would pull on Mademoiselle Karina's stockings, which went over me like a leotard. Lost way up in the intimate length of her, I slowly took root inside her. My heart bore the imprint of her soul. I crossed through her, to the other side of the looking glass. My penis unfolded like a roll of liquorice in the hands of a child. I had a massive erection. I rubbed against her shadow. At night, I wanted to follow her home and, with the moon for my accomplice, climb to the top of the ladder and surprise her naked. Steal other clothes of hers, her bra, without her knowing. That way, I would have possessed her completely. Climbing the creaking staircase without a sound, I would have slipped into her bed. I'd have liked to caress her belly, warm with a heavenly dew, and slowly sink into an incestuous dream between her luxuriant thighs. With my head buried in her white breasts, I'd have fallen asleep like a cradled child, listening to her heartbeat in my ear.

At dawn, my burrowing hands would carefully open her blouse and, with my lips and mouth, I would tickle her nipples for a while, until they hardened and grew erect as she slept. In the night of a lucid dream, I slept beside her. I stroked her buttocks, the small of her back. They were the constant emblems of the wild desire that appeared to flood them still. It seemed I was blessed with this miraculous love of a dwarf for a giant. Under the stars, I lost myself in her. I quivered with an instantaneous climax. I felt her shudder like an earthquake beneath me. At dawn, the path opened at our feet like the sea. We went off together down Romany road in a honeymoon caravan. Once I was awake, I struggled to keep the images of my reverie inside me; they'd slipped out of reach. Thanks to playing truant, I forgot everything I'd been taught, except the memory of Mademoiselle Karina's curves, which were engraved on me like a sketch by Rubens.

But how can I describe the flow of those days, one moment full of rage, the next full of wonder? It was quite natural that Bako and I should roam the streets together, dragging each other along. Life had wings. What bliss! We felt light, so light. This was the life. We'd have liked it to go on and on and never end.

I was the kind of kid who is always running away, who keeps running, along the rails that link the stars, hanging off cloud wagons. A mischievous little vagabond, I'd scramble over orchard fences and walls to get to the apple trees. When I'd eaten my fill I would fall asleep in the branches and dream. I belonged to that race of children who are chased down the streets, pursued even in their dreams. I was one of those little hoodlums with a bag full of delightful, terrible fantasies. I wandered the paths of the school drop-out. I loved images but not learning. I could see the inkwells topple over and the school turn into a lake of ink, where the head, the teachers and parents all swam desperately for their lives. I'd watch them all drown, while I rushed off to play truant. They capsized in a swell, in boats made from pages of exercise books. They sank in a black and blue sea, carried off by giant waves. From the bank I could hear their screams and the sound of mud rising from the heaving deep. I looked at my stained fingers, at the classroom clock, and off I went, leaving the shipwrecked victims behind, whistling in the wind that blew through my hair. I had the blue blood of nomads in my veins.

My heart thudded too hard; so disorientating that I was stunned. I was mad for girls, the insolent ones you'd run into in the streets. They weren't the shy type. They'd drench themselves in perfume, like those sophisticated women in the adverts of fashion magazines. Bako's swear words made them blush even more than the kisses we stole from them. We'd dive down side roads that soon led to the secret alcoves of a church. What innocent games we played, all in a dizzy rush. Our fingers touched, there were fumblings and the mute confessions of inflamed cheeks, before the bite of the first kiss.

Ah, lips thin as scars, where are the kisses of our children's mouths?

My eyes bathed in the swirling waters of pale marshes where those small sirens float, in the muddy depths where, now and then, young men beautiful like pearl fishermen dive down slowly. Lying flat on their backs, their long hair strewn through the water, white-faced Ophelias drift aimlessly beside an empty, oarless boat. The night sky moves slowly above their eyes. The boat slips off in a welter of flowers, leaving branches and foliage in its wake. The croaking of frogs and a damp-smelling wind rise from the shore of the pond. Shrouded in a greenish mist that chills their brows, my little sweethearts float along gently under the surge of night; their parted lips promise such happiness. The Siamese twin sisters we saw in the street every other day disappeared into the trembling shade of willows and water lilies, in the stirring leaves, under branches crossed with slanting light. They had a lightness of being, that of snow in crystalline dawns and frosted dew. The gentle breath of the wind sent ripples across the water. The current carried the boat into the shadows beneath the weeping willows where the tips of their lower stalks plunged into the green water, and the dazzling white water lilies fanned out.

It was at the Jean Vigo centre in Béçon-les-Bruyères that I met Bako. He had been placed there after his parents died. In the few schools that accepted us, we shared the same bench and we were often thrown out together. I loved his mischievousness, his childish antics, his endlessly amused smile, which brought to mind a malicious Cupid firing off poisoned darts in all directions. When I stared into his eyes, like Narcissus I saw my reflection, my double.

Everything you see in yourself is reflected in the people you meet. We were marked by the same sign. We helped each other and hurt each other, sharing the same sad days. But at that age, we carried our sorrows lightly, we were joyful and alive. It was much later that they hardened into anger, when the wind carried us high above ourselves. We were joined by a bond that went back to the beginning of childhood, the kind forged in the streets of blue-collar districts where our meeting was already foretold – by us and by the fate that throws people together. All that goes back a long way, to the days when we weren't yet what we were to become.

We lived together through days, months and years of drifting. Wandering the city on sleepless nights, we were sleepwalkers who brushed against the walls.

Equipped with a thin stick coated in glue, we would steal the offertory money from the priests during the Sunday morning service. We did the rounds of the churches in the suburbs on an old blue moped with a broken exhaust pipe. Before we sped off, I'd pray on the prayer mat that God couldn't see us, because in those days I still believed in everything. We would run out of the church like two little devils.

During those episodes of petty pilfering, our muted fear mingled with pleasure. It's a delicious feeling, to pull back a big rusty bolt, disappear down a dark corridor and break into a house, your ears alert for the slightest creak of the worm-eaten wood panels.

We'd ring all the door bells, change the names on letter boxes, write in chalk on the walls 'Whoever reads this is a wanker' or 'Tarik loves Sylvie' and draw hearts pierced end to end with arrows. We'd let down bicycle tyres, steal pens, toys, gloves, records, jumpers, trousers and jackets from Prisunic supermarket and sell them at Clignancourt flea market. High up on dormitory balconies we'd throw eggs at passers-by. We'd slip through the railings of the amusement park to avoid the entry fee. We'd get into cinemas via the emergency exits. I remember one of our finest spoils was a magnificent new bike with chrome handlebars. We took turns riding it down the streets. At that age you pedal till your legs give out. The sun seemed to vibrate in the rays from the sparkling wheels. That's how it was, our whole childhood: climbing railings, breaking down doors, taking shutters off their hinges, day and night. It could all have gone very wrong. Luckily we were supple, fast runners.

One day, we even stole our headmaster's wallet from his office, where we'd been banished, and went off for a cruise along the Seine on a tourist boat. We drank beer and smoked cigarettes. I wasn't very good at smoking yet, but Bako could already swallow the smoke and blow it out of his nostrils. We'd tell each other story after story, we were always in fits of helpless laughter. We talked about girls' pubic hair and the smell of their knickers. We'd go and hang around Trône funfair, to check out the merry-go-rounds. How I loved the smell of gunpowder in the shooting galleries, the tinkly old tunes, the girls' screams when cars collided on the dodgems and the warmth of a bag of chips in my hands. It was a wonderland. The little gypsy kids with runny noses, who were scrawny and always had their fingers up their nostrils, might have been our brothers. There were different coloured caravans and tents put straight up on the grass. Our mouths watered at the sight of kilos of chunky nougat, big fluffy candyfloss and red dripping toffee apples. Everything melted. Chaos spread across the fair. There were rows and rows of stands, crammed together from end to end. There was everything, from Hercules' display of strength and the blind fortune-teller, to the magician with his abracadabras, and they all smiled as we went by. The big wheel turned high above the square. The mournful carousel music drifted around us, melancholic and slow. Which of the glowing caravans could she be sleeping in, the stallholder's daughter we were both secretly in love with? We could hear the piercing groans of the organ that came from the carousel with wooden horses; far too expensive for us. There were loads of slot machines, dodgems, donkeys, pipe-pulling contests, aeroplanes with dragonfly wings and lights that made you dizzy.

Four athletes stood on a platform, puffing out their chests, squarely planted on their legs, with bulging muscles like Greek gods', who shouted challenges to the crowd.

'Roll up! Roll up! Be brave, try your luck,' shouted a man into his microphone. 'Who wants to test their strength against Hercules, Maciste, Samson and Tarzan? Who . . .' But the onlookers were wary.

Mixed with the smell of new grass, the aroma of sausages

wafted through the air from a stand by an old carousel on which the horses went up and down rhythmically. Carried away in their never-ending round, kids shouted to each other from one horse to the next with laughter and delight. We went home, our heads dizzy with noise and exhilaration.

Wherever we were, Bako would spend most of his time lighting matches, box after box of them. It was his passion. For hours he would watch the little orange flame flare at his fingertips, slowly consuming the little wooden stick . . . until it burnt him. He also liked to walk along walls, teetering over the void like a tightrope walker, or to open the doors of speeding trains onto the tracks. These games made him come alive. In the summer, sitting on a wooden bench under the cymbals of the sun, his eyes staring into the blue sky, Bako would flick his wrist delicately from left to right and right to left, catching the rays on the steel of his knife. For whole days he would play at blinding me with the flashes that bounced off it as if from a mirror. The light sparked off the glittering steel; one tiny star would spangle and leap onto my eyelashes. I'd look away, as if the naked blade had injured my eyes with a dazzling blaze, like the sudden gleam of a sabre. Sometimes it seemed as if it wasn't Bako's hand playing with the knife, but the knife playing with his hand. Leaning forwards, with his head up and eyes wide open, he would stare straight into the sun's rays without blinking. Although we had different personalities, he was like a brother born long ago. We'd hang around outside railway stations: Saint-Lazare, Lyon, Austerlitz. We never tired of watching the trains. People came and went. It was like an ants' nest.

I had borrowed from the library an old map which had countries' names embossed on it in curling letters. When it was quiet, in the gloom, my face framed in the flickering flame of a candle, I would trace my finger round the coastlines of unknown shores and let myself dream. I knew everything about my islands lost on the edge of the world.

I knew the temperature, the rainy season, the names of the flora and fauna. And when I didn't know, I'd make it up. Bako was crazy about the islands dream, the naked girls in the sunshine. Lying on our beds in the dorm, we furtively smoked cigarettes. We imagined a cargo ship drifting slowly from port to port and island to island. We had to get away . . .

Our nights were all the same; they brought no solace. At last one evening we shivered with anticipation, listening to the beating of our panic-stricken hearts. A threatening presence lay in wait behind the dormitory curtains. Were we dreaming or was it real? A silhouette suddenly appeared on the glass like Chinese shadow theatre. Its blurry contours stood out in the dark. By a quivering light, I saw it sitting on the chair. Oh childish bewitchment by the light of another world . . .

We waited a long time, feigning sighs and light snoring, and as soon as the youth worker had gone back to his room, we sprang up like corpses come back to life. Sheets crumple and crease, everything is quiet. The city sleeps peacefully. But it wasn't that easy getting out of the centre every night.

'Bako, let's go.'

'OK. Are we going far?'

'To the islands.'

Outside is all the enchantment of the full moon. Prowlers are already gathering in the streets and down dead-ends, watching and waiting. We tread furtively through the dormitory, between the beds, on tiptoe so as not to wake anyone, careful not to make the floorboards creak. Grimacing shadows, our clothes making us look like scarecrows. We're alone in the night that fills our fear with evil spirits . . .

In the rustle of the leaves on the trees, I see frightening eyes. We are in the middle of a dark, impenetrable forest, the branches echo with the hooting of owls. A forest haunted by the souls of warlocks from the dark lands of legend. Bako upsets some water on his way and wets my shoes. We're stuck in murky bogs, crossing this dormitory in short steps. But suddenly, on the top of a magic mountain, Bako spies an ancient tower beside a strange kingdom. Dizzying, steep slopes with rocky ridges, overrun with carnivorous plants, the undergrowth a tapestry of tropical flowers. A castle rises from the mist of a lake. Here we are at last . . . mouths and noses pressed against the glass, in silence. For a moment we saw the stars twinkle.

'Bako, you know what, they're the same ones you can see from the islands.'

And we climbed out the window. It was our fate, always to be running away. That's just the way it was. It wasn't to go anywhere. It was just for the illusion of leaving. Blackest night now, only the white glow of a solitary street lamp pierced the shadows; all the others had been smashed by rampaging kids. Cars were parked along the pavements and the road itself was deserted.

That night, we slept on a park bench with our feet tucked up under our jackets, sheltered by a clump of bushy trees in Jean-Roger-Caussimon Park. In the depths of our sleep, the dry creak of sails brushed our lashes: a Spanish galleon, crammed with ornately carved coffers full of gold and spices. At the mast, a massive, splendid black flag flapping. The captain's weather-beaten face appeared on the prow, a patch over his right eye. He paced the bridge, where the crew was busy with the rigging. All sails to the wind, we saw the ship glide over the dismal grey surface of the Seine. Briefly, she drifted along the bank by Suresnes bridge towards the lock, then veered right amongst the old barges piled with coal. At last she made sail for the open sea, heading for the Leeward Islands, her sails set for the shores of the world. The captain stood calmly on the poop deck and scanned the horizon through his telescope. The galleon disappeared. Having gathered up all the sorrows of the suburbs, she carried them away beyond sea and sun.

We woke in the park at dawn. Here and there, down dusty paths, blackbirds pecked at the ground, looking for a crust. Further on, a pigeon with dirty, straggly feathers strutted between the wooden benches, cooing. A muffled hum of cars rose from below the slope of the road and streamed away with the sound of a torrent. Up to their necks in a hole, two Arab workmen were energetically throwing over their heads great shovelfuls of earth which landed with a flat thud. A dull pain gnawed at my leg. The fresh morning air blew right through our clothes. That afternoon we wound up at Austerlitz station. People were jostling for space in the crush, soldiers in uniform, passengers weighed down with bags, rushing in all directions. We found the first train due to leave. It was the Biarritz train. We asked the woman selling newspapers if there was sea in Biarritz.

'Of course,' she said. 'Sea's lovely there.' She was shouting, stirring up the crowd around her. We didn't have enough money for a ticket. We got on in the middle of the second-class compartments. When the train pulled out, our hearts were racing. The noise of the wheels on the rails made the windows vibrate. The train plunged into daylight, jolting rhythmically. Faces pressed to the glass, we watched the grey suburban houses and factory chimneys go by. We went past trees and embankments in the rolling countryside. We kept a constant, anxious look-out for the guards. Hiding in the toilets, I could see the rails and axles through the hole. Standing in the corridor, uneasy, among the drunken Foreign Legionnaires slumped on the floor, tossed from side to side, we dreamed of the sea that leads to the islands. It was a long journey. We went to the bar and bought two sandwiches and a Coca-Cola to share.

The train ploughed on. Bako was lying on the floor, rolled up in his jacket. Sometimes the convoy would slow down and come to a squealing halt alongside a platform. It arrived at Biarritz station very late at night. Some passengers left the train; we tried to mingle with them. We asked the way to the sea. Our legs ached after all that time cooped up in the train. Alone outside the station, we took a taxi.

'Where do you want to go?'

'To the sea,' I answered.

The driver glanced at us suspiciously in his rear-view mirror. Half buried in his overcoat, he drove on. The streets were empty.

From time to time we passed another car. The taxi dropped us by the promenade. We paid with our last pennies; he took off again, heading back up to the centre of town.

There it was, stretched in a thin, gleaming arc on the rim of the horizon, sumptuous in its perfect curve, like an enormous dark eye. We looked at it, speechless. We heard its low roar, a sound that's endured since the world began. Time is but the merest breath in the murmur of the waves. The moon lingered over the lagoons. The sea spread out like a mirror of water, silvery with the glint of stars that quivered on the breakers, cradling the dying gasp of the currents of equinoctial tides. We took off our shoes, which were heavy with sand, delightedly sinking our bare feet into the warm, soft top layer. In the distance we could see the sweeping beam of the lighthouse. Not a soul in sight. The houses and outlines of boats looked like toys. A roller washed up an empty bottle that knocked against my feet. For a moment I thought of the genie from age-old Arab stories. Bako took off his clothes, carefully placing his big shoes on top of them, and walked towards the sea. I joined him. Naked in the white foam, we swam a long time together in the cold baptismal water. Our slow strokes carried us far from the beach. Whooping with laughter, we splashed each other like mad puppy dogs, spraying white droplets that exploded on the skin. Bako disappeared under the water, plunging to the depths. He resurfaced a little later, enjoying the feel of the waves lapping all over him, splashing and playing silly games, filling his mouth with water to spout at me. He even pissed in the sea . . .

'Just for the memory . . .' he said.

We emerged, naked and streaming, and ran back to sit on the edge of the beach. Bako rolled the joint we'd promised ourselves, saying nothing, staring into the middle distance. We passed the pipe of peace between us; each inhalation merged with the breath of the tide. I smoked till I could hardly see. The sea filled my eyes; the breeze made it quiver and undulate slowly. I felt time slip between my fingers and the sand. I was suddenly overwhelmed with a sadness that came from the big blue, in this oppressive, empty landscape, as if I was lost in the middle of a desert, trembling and forgotten by the world. I didn't dare move. Our ruffled hair flew about in the night breeze. We walked barefoot along the shore; each wave dug a well around our heels and the sand got between our toes.

It was chilly. Tired out, we slept back to back, wrapped up in our jackets, in the hull of a boat, a wreck full of shells. A high wind rose in spirals from the earth to the clouds and blew across the beach, scattering sheaves of sand up through the air. Big black clouds gathered on the horizon. Suddenly, the growl of a storm rolled through the skies and the heavens opened. The squall slapped the city ramparts, shattering the glass in slamming windows. The lightning detonated in a mighty flash. Giant waves unfurled, swollen by the tide, foaming, furious and massive, wet with iridescent pearls. Infinity rolled at our feet. Waves surged over villa walls, rising and falling where sea and sky drowned in a swell streaked with long trails of white. The sky was the colour of cold ash. House walls gave way under the water pressure. Cars floated; the whole city surrendered to the flood. Sheets of water carried everything away. Creatures emerged from the deep. In the fury of the tornado, blood-spattered sea birds, squawking wildly, crashed into the black rocks, flapping their wings. Ships rocked on the crests of waves, wounded ghost ships about to founder. Rats streamed out of gaping cracks where water rushed in. The points of their sharp teeth fastened onto the torn rigging and sails. Women and men clung desperately to the wreckage; the ocean rose faster and faster. The world was sinking, carried away by deep waters. Snow ran in torrents from mountaintops to the bottom of valleys. Only one frail child, hanging from the claws of a royal eagle, was saved from the shipwreck. Pure water cleansed the earth, washing away everything from the sand, and I saw the birth of the world's dawn in its shimmering purity as a starlit, untouched new land. All that was left was all there will be one day, just lagoon and sand.

A hand shook me awake in the cold of dawn. A thin mist filled the sky and the dunes. The rising tide lapped at my shoes. I shivered, rubbing my thighs, which were numb with sleep. Already a fishing boat was gliding silently in the distance. Like a faintly feverish pulse, I felt a sudden clank of metal on metal, then a cold click. A pair of handcuffs round my wrists.

'So, slept well, you little scumbag?'

I saw their blank, hostile faces. I felt terrible, my hair was full of sand and dry seaweed and my lips stung with salt. There was no one on the beach. No one but the policemen, the sea and us . . . Bako shuddered in the cold wind. The policemen took us back through the streets, handcuffed to their wrists. At daybreak a magnificent sun rose over the city. I turned back to look at the sea. Now boats thronged the port. A sail on the horizon fluttered like a wing in the breeze. As we entered the police station, a plain-clothes inspector in his fifties called out: 'Ah. The two little twits.'

The man started asking questions in a harsh voice, and from time to time he looked me straight in the eye. I tried to hold his gaze. His mouth was full of threats and hate, but I knew we'd run away again one day, we'd go even further and never come back.

Bako was watching me. He didn't say a word. I saw his tired face; we hadn't eaten since the day before. He was weak and disappointed; the islands were too far. Salty tears brimmed on his lashes and slid down to the corners of his mouth. You can never tell where or when grief will end. Maybe at the end of the world. It takes a lifetime of remembering, maybe even longer.

Perhaps Bako already knew what was coming, the long nights of waiting in cells with no daylight. But I was only thinking of tomorrow's escapades, the exhilarating winds and the white pebbles we had scattered along the seashore.

From then on we just lived in anticipation of sudden departures, like those heavy-winged birds that fly out there in the distance, to the end of the sky. They know there are no trees or places to rest.

So often we were led in handcuffs to the police station, sharing the cage with adults, waiting to appear before the juvenile court judge. Then, down dirty, dimly lit corridors at night, we were moved to a cell on the first floor, which had a bunk bed, mattresses, blankets, lice and crabs, no water but a light kept on permanently. How many hours we spent there, punctuated by the jangle of keys opening and closing cells. That was how the spell was broken. For us, the tribulations of childhood always ended in the juvenile cells.

Was this wicked fate the result of our misdemeanours? I don't know. Nothing in life is fair, neither happiness nor sadness. The craziness begins with a sense of impending disaster, the giddiness you sometimes feel when you realise you don't know yourself at all, nor this world you're passing through, where you don't belong. Life was there, ever-present, always the same, worn and twisted. Inevitably, as the days went on, you got used to it, you started to resemble it.

We came across so many shadows, so many faces blurred into others, long forgotten – that is, if they'd ever even existed. But the true meaning of every encounter would be revealed in time. Everyone in their own way pushed us towards wild excess.

The car cruised the streets, windows down. A gust of wind blew in and swelled our shirts. Right foot pressed on the accelerator, a glance in the wing mirrors, Pascal stared at the road ahead. His jittery hand went up through the gears with a kind of solemnity. Huddled together in the back, we powered on, waving our hands from the open windows. The car drove fast. Speed limits didn't bother us. Leaning forward, Pascal slammed his foot down on the accelerator as though to break through the car floor. He had a leather band round his right wrist, where a snake, coiled round a dagger, reared its head. A lock of his thick black hair, greased back with brilliantine, kept flopping onto his forehead. The needle on the dial veered to the right. We streaked ahead in a flash of pink, orange and white.

The city quivered in the lights. The Porsche's headlights ploughed tunnels down the long avenues. The glazed asphalt glittered in a drizzle of rain. It would have been madness to get in our way at the speed we were travelling, in that molten steel shell that stank of petrol and gas. We didn't know where we were going, but we were going fast, that was what mattered. We wanted to drive like that for miles, wherever the road took us, oblivious of ourselves and everyone else. To get to the end of something, head towards someone, just for the illusion that maybe someone somewhere was waiting for us.

We'd found the car in a residential neighbourhood. The door wasn't locked. No alarm. All we had to do was sink into the red leather seats. Pascal caressed the steering wheel with both hands; just the old wiring trick and the ignition light was on. The petrol gauge pointed to full. We could have gone to the ends of the earth like that, with the engine softly throbbing, crossing borders, mountains, houses, walls, sky and stars, for days and nights on end. Cigarette lighter, adjustable seats, radio and tapes. The straight and narrow they always nagged us about, this was the kind we should keep to, averaging 180 km an hour. There was barely time to grow old on such journeys, which form young lives.

What did we care for the useless research of experts, scanning the sky for signs of the end of time? We knew ours wasn't far off. We could hear it like dogs pulling sledges hear the crack of the whip at their ears. We shared their fate. We could feel time suspended as in the substance of the man who instinctively knows when to bring it all to an end. No point being sad. Men are born and die. From the break of day to the close of night, each of us drags his wounds around, licking them in secret until the day he can no longer bear the fetid stink that oozes out of them.

Ensconced in his seat, Pascal pulled off some stylish high-performance stunts for us. Taking the corners wide, doing controlled skids and brilliant half-spins in the night. We wanted amazing adventures, not to eke out the days in one long yawn of boredom. Something had to happen. Even the worst. Nothing was too reckless for Pascal. He rejected sleeping dreams. He wanted to live them, eyes wide open. Although he was only sixteen, he could have taken on racing drivers. He had that buzz about him, that tense vibrancy. While others slept the sleep of the just, we raced like wildcats through the city. We sped off, weaving our way through the streets like snakes, grazing bumpers, skimming parked cars on the corners and scraping their wings. Pascal stuck out his tongue as he drove, like a kid on a merry-go-round. His front teeth gave him a squirrel-like smile. He could drive a car at 200 km an hour and stop it dead at the foot of a wall, turn it down tight alleys at 100, reverse at full speed and do a hand-brake stop so sharp the car would jolt as he jumped from his seat, or engage the clutch as he slammed the door and roared off down the street.

He surrendered to the thrill of high speed as if he knew that one day age would count for nothing. That it would just be a matter of getting old, submitting to time. So you had to try to go faster than time itself. I can't remember much about Pascal. Through the written word, in ink, his features come back as in clear water. Some people are like stars. Carried along by their own momentum, they blaze through the sky without stopping. Could his smile, pure as ice, have been extinguished in the warm breath of an exhaust pipe, trailing acrid smoke like a long black veil?

A few of us hung out near a wasteland where rusty car engines were thicker on the ground than grass in the fields, and we'd kick up one hell of a din in the burnt-out shells. The older boys would bring a retarded girl to an abandoned wooden shed, under the tarred paper roof, among piles of old tin cans and greasy rags. She let them have their way, out of habit. It didn't even occur to her to run away. She made little animal whimpers and left as she'd come, shaken and twitchy, hugging the walls, pink blood trickling from her bare, scratched thighs. So many girls lost their virginity like that, there or in some basement, one after the other.

Sometimes, one of them would bring a baby into the world without thinking. They did it alone, like dogs . . . But who did it look like? Us, maybe. At the bottom of stairwells with no lifts, young girls appeared with fragile hips and golden hair. In the unlit basements of the tower blocks, in the flickering light of a candle, we'd push them down on ripped mattresses and nibble at their small white breasts. We'd lie curled up together a long time, our eyes shining, the darkness punctured only by the glowing tip of the cigarette we passed between us.

Every inner-city estate had its own gang of bad boys; Pascal belonged to the Pâquerettes gang. That was where we'd met him.

Up there, among the scrap merchants, behind the council blocks that line the road, in that area exuding olive oil, live angels with toothless grins, thin kids with a mysterious radiance. Dribbles of snot hung from their nostrils. Lone children walked the streets in baggy clothes. Hair spiked, eyes hard as metal, wide open in the shadows like frightened cats.

On the pavements, adolescent boys shout and strut their macho stuff, half-open mouths proffering obscene viper tongues to the girls, who keep on walking but still glance over at them. They lick their hands and drag them down the length of their torsos, stroking themselves. They burst out laughing when the girls blush. Their laughter echoes from one end of the street to the next, their voices blend together. Every few seconds they run a greasy comb through their hair, to get the wave at the back right, and strike scornful poses.

At the back of Chez Bébert, the old bar, a chrome jukebox held pride of place, all gleaming plastic and electricity; the needle slowly sets off, slides over the record, stops and settles in the first groove of the chosen track. We'd clap our hands in the air, in time with the staccato beats of the music. I can see us now, sitting on the staircase steps, spewing out swear words as arcane to us as erudite literary jargon. In those days, we couldn't put three sentences together without a torrent of filth pouring from our mouths, and our curses weren't pig Latin. 'Shut your face, arsehole . . . If pricks paved the street, that bitch you call your muvva, would use her cunt as feet . . .' we'd sing out – us, the choirs of the Red suburbs – at dumbfounded passers-by.

Ignorant kids we were, amazed to discover words in reverse. There was no fun to be had in going straight ahead; we beat a path on the flipside of things. In the impossible task of trying to describe our lives, all I can think of is that language picked up on the street, that back-slang that's slung back like us, all crooked. Any one of us could have been something else, we just should have been born elsewhere. Our eyes burnt with a strange, dark flame; they gleamed with light. Weird signs marked our skin: crosses, stains shaped like arrows and names, engraved like the intertwined initials of childhood days. Our necks, arms and torsos were emblazoned with this sacred heraldry, dots of ink that we paraded like jewels, smeared with blood and crossings-out, knights' coats of arms, in silver and azure, with gold-tongued lions' jaws – royal titles for pavement princes. Our evil ways accentuated our beauty, like something indecent. In our shining eyes, all this laughing insolence turned to sensual joy.

Life succumbs to repetition, unto infinity. The dream was still the same as in the days of those first inner-city bad boys distinguished by a gold ring in one ear, who defended the territory. Lives all alike, they were dead having barely lived. Violence was everywhere in the narrow, dirty streets.

A long way from the green baize and the roulette wheels of casinos, lit by the pale glow of a streetlight, are one cardboard box and three cards. Chancing your luck on two reds and winning black: 'Watch carefully . . . I'll shuffle again . . . Watch carefully . . .' At the end of the street, tense with the strain of being look-outs, Bako and I would signal the sudden approach of police patrols. The cardboard box was folded up and vanished into the night. Sometimes, over an insult, we'd fight, then get up again, fists hammering face and stomach, a sound of crushed cartilage and broken bones under the skin. A man yelled something from a window. He'd barely disappeared before a siren wailed and the patrols began, black cars with rotating lights flashing orange and blue. The footsteps of shadows echoed as they fled from one pavement to the next. Other times, boys leaped out like wild things and tangled in virile sparring matches. These were feral hand-to-hand combats, a happy circle of barbarians. They were handsome like oblivious gods, planting delicious unease in healthy souls. They were so proud, the slightest pity seemed an insult to their beauty. There was a kind of haughtiness in their movements. Naked, adorned in their sacred regalia, burning all over, their bodies rippled like cats. Their lonesome eyes glittered and cut like diamonds. They would burst onto wastelands where little dark-haired raggedy girls play, round the blocks of flats where barefoot boys run after a black and white ball, watched by stray cats with torn ears that they'd sometimes chase, throwing stones, between the dusty trees. There, where foul water flows in the gutters and rubbish piles up, the remains of feasts: stale crusts of bread, eggshells, bones, chicken carcasses, broken glass, rusty supermarket trolleys. They pass through the filth of bloodied white clothing and dead cat foetuses, at the edge of the dump where rats and evil flourish.

They emerge from the shadows, slip down winding roads at the foot of the walls, into doorways, up steps, in underground car parks, over the flower-filled balconies of white villas, the balustrades of apartments, onto the roofs of department stores. They climb up and down, they run, they twist and turn. They don't walk. They float in the heavy air. They ignore statues, road names, monuments, those posing for posterity, still alive – their arms and legs are covered in a green sheen like the old bronze statues in the park. What's the point of waiting till you're a broken old man leaning on a cane, shoulders slumped with a weariness that slowly gives way under your feet like shifting sand? They saw a great fall, a spewing out of everything and everyone.

It is a lightning flash which defines their rapid youth – the burst of a breaking storm, the thunderbolt that kills tree and child. A spark sets them alight, illuminating them with a resplendent beauty amid the golden stars and shattered sky. They passed by the sun, and blew it out like a candle. Now their faces are death masks. One by one I lost them in the darkness. Stones, streets and monuments will not honour their names. A night of drunkenness and fornication in a city somewhere. Wherever, in some godforsaken place, a seduced, abandoned woman will give birth to a boy or a girl. She won't even know the father's name. Another lover will recognise the child in law. The fathers won't remember; they're just passing through. It was some night with a girl they picked up on the road. That's how it goes. No one notices.

Nothing born of them will carry their names. They themselves have never tried to find out the name of whoever fathered them. The words that come out of their mouths seem to have no echo, their lives no continuation. They seem to have been raised not by men but by vanished beings, used to a life with no horizons, as if they'd been conceived in the smell of the air and flies' eggs, on ground that crawls with all the things that do not last. They only become visible to your reality on the pages of the tabloids. They are set apart from the living, already carved in stone used for epitaphs.

Round here, shifty-looking rogues and ragamuffins took to peddling fake old coins, gold chains and other junk made by their partners in rue des Lombards. They also played with loaded dice, with safe-breakers and crooks from out of town who sneaked into the city disguised as dealers. Despite private guards and the local police force, they carried out some daring thefts in rue Vieille-du-Temple, rue du Bourg-l'Abbé, rue de l'Écu-Doré. The skeletons of impenitent thieves, swallowed up by the voracious soil, lay beneath the rue de la Truanderie where we hung out. That's where the gravediggers had piled them up. To find these heaps of bones in old Paris, an excavation on All Souls' Day was all that would have been needed. Souls flowered beneath our feet.

That was our world, and it'll probably be the same in ten thousand years; other people will walk, as we did, over a charnel house, on this land where people have erred from dawn to gloomy dusk. In time's mirror, yesterday's dead would recognise themselves in the faces of today's. Decline rules this rabid world, rotten with vermin, where tooth and nail is all you've got to fight with, a decline still medieval in its blood and gold.

When we invented the wheel, we tied a man to it; at the first forge, we burnt him. And that's how it has been down the centuries of human thinking. A trail of fire, from gunpowder to fuse, a universal carousel of smouldering fury. The earth is trapped in a circle of flames. The same merry-go-round starts up again, the anguish repeating itself like a madman's twitch. Centuries of war haven't stopped war; they've just moved it an inch further round the globe. In spite of all the faces blown off, stomachs slit open, skulls smashed, the yells, screams, gasps, death rattles, and in spite of the charnel houses. Do we have to be dead, then, to feel something like peace? Couldn't we live peacefully in a country hidden away somewhere, beyond the torment of men, under a clear sky, even for a day?

Under the arches of old hovels, on roof corners, the taverns' rusty signs could still be seen slamming in the wind: 'The White Horse', 'The Golden Trough'. Foul-mouthed rascals, quarrelsome and violent, quick to offend, came there to lose their souls, to curse and drink, entertain the pretty girls and run after barmaids. But most of them would come to while away the night. Devilishly dressed and armed with daggers, they fell on passing gents. In the Middle Ages, four gallows rose at the four main gates into Paris. One of them was in Les Halles, where there were also stocks, for thieves or blasphemers. Today, a police station stands in the same place, where Bako and I were sometimes held for pilfering.

A gang of kids slept rough near the fountain of the Innocents. They were cheeky and debauched, humble and full of pride, sensitive, malicious and pathetic, candid and perverse at the same time, frivolous and solemn. Lost children who roamed through life, like that poet of yesteryear who, on the Montfaucon gallows, squeezed out a jarring tune, as a limpid tear trembled like a dewdrop on the tip of his cock. So many necks were snapped on ropes too tight. Suspicious shadows prowled the narrow streets, beggars and thieves flouting order and custom. They could die of grief and life would leave them there, broken and bloody at the foot of a wall. Nothing is ever said about what dogs have seen, or what the poor have died from. You have to walk the streets to see what they have in common: a cortège of blurred, distorted shapes emerges from underground tunnels, rushes through Beaubourg like a herd of wild beasts, squealing and bellowing through the streets in a rolling, echoing howl. From all over town, shadows loom, supernatural creatures surge from dark ravines. Yesterday's chamber of horrors merges with today's, arrayed along the wall. Some dissolve like melted statues to the ground. Bodies slump gently in a heap of rags. They are broken and no one thinks to pick them up. They are trampled in a dizzy rush. And so they stay like that, motionless on the ground, until the chill of the night numbs their legs, their arms, their heads.

The well-to-do of Beaubourg are repelled by the emaciated, ragged drunks who drift past, convulsed with coughing fits and bad wine; clearing their throats between spasms, spitting on the ground and swearing. Their voices are croaky, rasping from the cough that rips at their insides. Some of them are stretched out on a hot-air vent, huddled on the ground, benumbed, skin haggard, faces chalk-white. The local residents are haunted by these pockmarked faces with their insipid hot breath and the decayed, scabby flesh they leave behind them. They're afraid they'll get infected with these diseases one day, like those which peasants contracted in the past, in lowly brothels, from scurrilous harlots and charmless matrons with sagging breasts.

It was during such ill-fated days that we sensed the first signs of a calamity in the air which would sow the seeds of disaster. Some already hailed it as a plague sent by God . . .

Les Halles: overrun by homeless vagabonds and hirsute gangs who watched and waited on dangerous street corners until dawn. That was where we met Sikko and Luc. They could also be found in one of those small alleyways that penetrate the old neighbourhoods, wandering from one bar to the next. They spent whole days there. Sikko and Luc lived in Macadam Squat, near place d'Italie, in an old abandoned building. Dust whirled in the winter wind. Cans and bottles of beer lay in piles of rubbish. Cardboard replaced broken glass in the windows. Inside this ruined world, they lived like rats under a heap of debris. The pitted walls were sprayed in multi-coloured graffiti, like kids' drawings; the comic-strip characters gave the place a party atmosphere. They lived off occasional menial work and petty thieving. Luc spent his days reading detective novels and drinking cans of beer. Sikko, known as 'the half-caste', boxed a little. He was a proper heavyweight with the natural agility of a middleweight, and he had trouble keeping his innate aggression in check. He was short and stocky, his nose was broken, and his head sank into his shoulders. What made him scary was the intensity of his little grey eyes.

Outside the ring, he spent his time repairing an old 1960s Aronde. Although they were both a lot older than us, it made us more than proud to be accepted and protected by them. Luc had a gift for putting anyone at ease; he was curious about people and things, more knowledgeable than he looked, and we were soothed by his way with words. There was an indisputable authority about him; we obeyed him instantly. Anyone would have trusted him.

Luc had heard stories of lavish country houses where masked costume balls and debauched orgies worthy of Louis XIV's brother were held. He told us in minute detail what our roles in the proceedings would be, among people who liked the company of adolescent boys. We were totally reassured when he explained what he had in mind for the evening. The following week we cased the joint, trying to avoid times when our comings and goings might have been noticed. It was impressive, this property, with its courtyard shaded by lime trees. Wearing a big hat, the gardener pruned roses in the garden. We glimpsed him at the end of the gravel paths, in the shade of the leaves. Sikko had unearthed a pink jacket and a frilly shirt from somewhere, Luc had a top hat, a long black cape and white gloves. Bako was dressed as a knight with me as a page – black thigh boots, red leather waistcoat and a billowing shirt. We had all chosen our own costumes.

This unsettling game exhilarated me. I was still drifting along in life, in an escape frozen in time. I'd always been a fantasist. In my dreams, I would wander amid golden embroidery, the rustle of old silk, captivated by perfumes and jewels, during a time when such finery was the norm. Dressed up, perfumed, their faces made up for rare pleasures, in subdued light, I'd imagine sweet young girls in pink silk masks, veils, and cascades of floating muslin. I dreamed of a leg brushing against mine, the peppery aroma of a breast. I saw myself lost in the twists and turns of a maze, running with other boys to look for an unknown girl and getting it all wrong, of course.

During this game no one could show their face or reveal their identity, while playing it or afterwards, so that night alone would know its mysteries. Pleasure should be a sacred secret. Gentle, half-naked Aphrodites would appear, through transforming mirrors, in bridal veils and flounces, strolling in stiletto heels sharp enough to pierce a dreamer's heart. Elegant women, their faces concealed behind sequinned fans, white roses in their hair, materialised before me. Cloak-and-dagger films had left their indelible mark. I was almost always in my fantasy world, glimpsing these delights. The great, naive legends of my childhood came to life before my eyes; the tournament knights in their red cloaks, gold spurs, azure and silver buckles, with feet in stirrups, proudly parading their harness and their plumes . . .

Luc lowered the window of the Aronde. He had covered the licence plate the night before. He bathed his face in the rush of icy night air. We'd just left the outskirts of Nanterre. The car sped softly down the road. Hardly anyone was about at that hour and nothing was open except a few petrol stations with their forlorn little lights. We crossed Le Vésinet with its stately properties where, according to Luc, a film actor had invested his gold. The road seemed endless. In the glove box there was a bottle of Johnny Walker, half full. Sikko grabbed it, opened it, sniffed it and put it to his lips, then passed it to Luc. He took a large swig.

'Five kilometres to go,' he murmured. 'If we make a packet tonight, I'll take you to the Golden Dragon, where they have geishas: real women, delicate, refined, welcoming like flowers. Vietnamese women all in silk. You lie down and they massage you from head to toe, in a bath with white tiles—'

'That isn't a bath . . . it's a fountain of dreams,' Sikko interrupted. His angular face, sharp as a blade, suddenly came alive.

The moon appeared at the rim of the sky. The radio was turned down low. The metal carcass protected us. On the back seat with Bako, I was still listening to Luc dream out loud. He seemed invulnerable. I wondered how he managed not to show any of the excitement he must have felt as we approached our destination. It's true the haunting atmosphere of his stories stayed with us a long time, till the end of the ride. His dream pursued us in a blaze of red and gold fire: an enchanted palace with enamelled roofs, bursting with baroque luxury, fluttering multi-coloured banners and flowery paper lanterns. There were dragons, phoenixes, unicorns – all the leering divinities of legend. I was intrigued by the revolver that bulged at Sikko's hip. He had no holster for it, and the purple reflection on the barrel gleamed like a threat, imposing defined limits on life . . . I had seen men killed in films, but I'd never had any contact with firearms before. I was seized with the urge to experience the sensation people feel when they shoot, the acrid smell of burnt powder that fills the lungs when the finger grips the trigger and a jet of orangey blue flame flares out. I was indulging these wild thoughts when Sikko twiddled the knob on the radio. A melancholy piece of music came out: 'It's a Man's, Man's, Man's World'. Sikko turned it up; he loved that song. The empty bottle of whisky lay at his feet. I could feel his exhilaration, full of a weird tension. We pulled the car over to the side of the road at a petrol pump. The advertising signs creaked in the wind. The pump attendant was reading a detective story in the booth, a big Alsatian stretched out at his feet. It pricked up its ears at us but didn't budge.

'Fill her up' was all Luc said.

We set off again. Red, amber and green lights flashed at the junction. There were few passers-by.

At the top of the hill, just after a short stretch of woodland, Sikko murmured: 'We're here, guys.' The headlights revealed a tree-lined avenue that led to the property. The car slowed down and moved cautiously. Sikko parked by a wall and switched off the lights. The mansion was white, with high stained-glass windows overlooking the park. A circular lawn with grass that was softer than velvet led down to a small river. Expensive cars were parked in the drive. The gravel crunched underfoot. I shivered with cold. The sensible thing would have been to leave then, at once, but it was probably already too late. The house looked massive in the moonlight. Alone, none of us would have dared go anywhere near such a place, or climb these walls; we were well aware we didn't belong to the same world and weren't even the same species as the people they enclosed.

I remember hoping no one would come to the door. I don't know why but I had a horrible feeling of foreboding. I suddenly got cramps which slowed me to a shuffle. Secretly I was afraid. I wondered what I was doing there, I should never have come. I wanted to run away.

A paved marble terrace loomed at the end of the drive. Once we were outside the door Sikko listened carefully but couldn't hear anything. He gave three sharp raps, then another, then knocked again, following the code for guests. Silence. I could hardly breathe. We waited for a moment in the darkness, then a shutter slid halfway open.

'Eros,' whispered Luc. That was the password. A hand opened the door with a special key which activated an electronic bolt. We were ushered in. A servant led us into a small living room that looked onto the greenery in the park.

'I'll fetch Madame,' he said and closed the door softly. The room was decorated with impressive Chinese furniture and heavy Persian rugs lay over the impeccably polished parquet floor. Sikko sank into the sofa as though he owned the place.

The mistress of the house appeared. She was wearing a mask, black veils and a red leather bra. She was accompanied by two young girls in transparent underwear and Peter Pan collars. They were frivolous and hysterical; they couldn't stop giggling. The woman ordered them to be quiet and to switch off the two chandeliers that hung from long beams across the ceiling.

'Follow me,' she said haughtily. She had an affected tone of voice. A gold chain encircled her thick waist. She walked in front of us like a priestess on her way to perform a black mass, high heels clicking down an endless corridor. We went down a spiral staircase, almost losing our balance several times. Bako held onto the banister.

Once we were in the basement, the woman pushed open three doors in quick succession. The last opened onto a subterranean room, some kind of salon for secret ceremonies, arrayed with baroque bronzes, gilded angels, Aphrodites, Salomes and winged nymphs, naked slaves carved in ebony; the sculptures were prominently displayed on ivory plinths. All these mirrors, all the gold and the chandeliers frightened me. The place had been created for orgies on a grand scale. It was like a painful dream, staring at so much naked flesh; men, women, girls and boys lying all over the place; it was agonising. On the floor piles of photographs lay scattered in dozens on the carpet. The atmosphere was heavily homosexual. The paintings on the walls depicted pubescent youths of antiquity indulging in the voluptuous pleasures celebrated in Alexander's Greece. I saw my own image reflected to infinity in the mirrors that covered the walls and ceiling. I stared at myself for a long time, as though in a dream. Perhaps, I said to myself, we'd disappear as easily as we'd come. My eyes wandered over all those bodies before alighting on a copper cross that hung from the wall, a bizarrely twisted Christ nailed to it, among shepherds and sheep, shepherdesses and saints, perched like birds on laurel branches.

The music was deafening. Men and boys sheathed in leather and chains danced and embraced each other lewdly through wreaths of smoke . . . Others, bulging and fat, kitted out in suspender belts over hairy legs, their lips daubed subtle reds, drank champagne and laughed uproariously. A woman danced, all but naked in a close-fitting net of silver threads. A man was piercing her breast with a hat pin, in ecstasy. What some asked from sensual pleasure, others obtained from the stinging bites of a lash across the back and thighs. It was like a nest of hissing vipers.

A young girl of about fifteen leaned on her hands with her legs apart, her head thrown back and skirt pulled up, offering herself to a withered old man with a skeletal frame and a bald head. He pulled his cold, cadaverous penis and ejaculated, letting out the little groans and shrill cries of a rutting pig.

We glimpsed the eyes of these eminent libertines behind their masks, made up and dressed like noblemen, powdered like waxy lords, adorned by dishevelled hairpieces, hanging on the arms of vulgar women wearing dresses that showed off their breasts, decorated with beauty spots. Three women, clad in leather outfits bristling with straps and hooks, were touching and stroking each other, embracing, separating, entwining and fusing in the to-and-fro motion of a pendulum, emitting hoarse, whining gasps. One of them appeared equipped with that which is the pride of men, an exact copy of a phallus, with all its attributes, made of some kind of rubber that was stiff and pliable. Erect between her thighs it swayed slowly before her as she moved. Sikko scanned the room. A perceptive onlooker might have seen the hatred in his steady gaze. It was a long while before he summoned enough composure to say:

'Now.'

His voice brought us back to reality. He suddenly lashed out, landing a kick in the stomach of an old man who spat out his dentures, sending them flying through the air. The old man wheezed as he picked them up. His tears smelled like rotten flowers forgotten in a vase.

Sikko grabbed the mistress of the house by the hair and pointed his gun at her head. She screamed.

'Shut your mouth, you old slapper.'

He punched her in the ear. Half-stunned, she went quiet. Luc waved his pistol at the other people.

'Cut the phone lines,' he told us, 'and collect the jewellery. Hand over your possessions,' he added, a note of impatience in his voice.

Wedding rings, signet rings, earrings, chains, lighters, watches, diamonds, credit cards, chequebooks, cash, crocodile skin wallets. The entire contents of the place Vendôme lay before us.

'How nice to be rich,' said Sikko sarcastically.

'Listen, I really can't get my wedding ring off. You see, I've been wearing it for twenty years.'

'No problem, ma'am,' Luc replied. 'We'll chop off your fingers and, if you like, we'll do your nails afterwards . . . Have no fear, I'm an expert manicurist.'

To prove the point, Bako took out his flick-knife. The woman did as she was told.

'Who, pray, is the owner of this fine establishment?' Luc asked.

'This house is mine,' said a man in a posh voice, casually detaching himself from the group. He was tall and elegant, with a red silk scarf tied nonchalantly round his neck. He stepped forward, naked from the waist down.

'Very good. Be so kind as to take us to your bedroom; you must have some family heirlooms about the place. Unless, of course, you're an orphan.'

'Your masks are quite delightful,' spat the owner, 'but black leather jackets would be more your style.'

'We'll keep that in mind for next time, my prince. Meantime, please do as I say.'

At gunpoint, the man began to walk. Sikko kept the others at bay.

After climbing fifty or so steps, we reached a huge, lavish room. As we entered, a draught made the curtains flap. We were in the man's private space, and he didn't seem to appreciate the intrusion. I noticed the exceptional furniture in the room, ringed by sofas upholstered in silk. There were oriental rugs, English-style furniture, old-fashioned velvet armchairs, paintings by old masters. The place was littered with trinkets, Chinese porcelain vases, an assortment of disparate objects. A contrived disarray prevailed in the overall design of the place, its opulence displayed with artful carelessness and a lofty scorn for bad taste. A suit had been left on the bed. The staff had clearly been given the day off.

We brazenly rummaged through drawers, cupboards and wardrobes. It was a brutal violation right under the man's eyes, a stab at the heart of his privilege. Near the window, dozing on a white piano, a plump Persian cat stared at us strangely. An antique bronze statuette and a magnificent silver gilt candlestick were displayed on the mantelpiece.

We threw everything into a canvas bag. Tucked away under a pile of embroidered napkins, at the bottom of a drawer, we unearthed the family silver. We blithely went about our business. Bako grabbed a fistful of jewels from a pretty ebony box. I became the proud owner of an ivory chess set, a real museum piece. The man still had his hands in the air; the threat of the revolver Luc pointed at the side of his head kept him quiet. He watched bitterly as we stripped him of his lawful possessions.

Outside, a breeze caressed the sleepy garden; the curtains rippled at the windows. I couldn't stop that trembling of the heart that occurs every time you push open the door of a flat without warning, making the hinges squeak, or gently force the wood of a chest of drawers which groans and twists with a soft crack that breaks the silence. My eyes darted round the room. The man's wealth had brought him plenty of things. In the bookcase I found numerous beautiful leather-bound volumes, the titles in thin gold lettering. I pulled them out and the rows of books collapsed. There was a score on the music-rest of the grand piano, open at the page of a Chopin nocturne. On walls draped with tapestries, below a high ceiling, hung a painting bright with scarlet reds, cobalt blues and regal, ecclesiastic purples. Opening the door to another room, I found a sunken bath, level with the floor, with fabulous Italian taps. In the bedroom, next to a canopied double bed, was a Louis XVI writing desk and a chaise-longue covered in silk. A feverish agitation kept me in the room. An opium pipe rolled in my hands. I could see the wreaths of clandestine smoking. I felt the sensual magnetism of the objects in my palms. Their history seeped into me. A shiver ran through my body, like that of a holy man suspended in mid-fervour, holding in his hands a bleeding cross. Bako was everywhere at once, exploring each corner of the room. Nothing escaped his eagle eye. Quick to find things, he was in no hurry. He made a big fuss over the smallest discovery. In the drawer of the bedside table I found a little silver-encrusted revolver, a marvel of Swiss workmanship. I played with it for a moment, feeling the weight of it in my hand. I made as if to fire, and took aim at Bako, who put up his hands, an amused glint in his eye.

'Getting warm, warmer, you're burning!'

He seemed to forget himself in his antics and childish games. He didn't realise we should stop now and leave. He flitted around the room like a sparrow. A sudden nightmare vision froze my throat. I saw the man, mad with fury, lunge like a mastiff at Bako. Taken by surprise, Luc didn't move, his gun was aimed at nothing. Small beads of sweat gleamed on his forehead. I panicked. Despite his shock, Bako managed to spin round and instinctively stuck the point of his flick-knife into the man's chest. Swept along by his own momentum, the man's forehead smashed into the corner of a Louis XV chest of drawers and he slid onto the rug, sinking the blade in up to the hilt. As he fell I heard a slight rattle, like the sigh of a sleeping man turning over in bed. He made a huge effort to get up, but his knees buckled and all his muscles failed him. He fell to his knees, swayed again and stretched out his arms, shaking with trembling convulsions. Already his life was just a vague memory. In one breath, he let his head fall back on the parquet floor.

Bako looked at me, his face livid and distorted. He was

shaking all over and his teeth were chattering. He covered his face with one hand. He blinked, as if he couldn't believe what he saw. He closed his eyes and rubbed them with the tips of his fingers. For a long time all three of us stayed like that, stock-still, in an icy silence. At last, Luc approached the body and turned it over. Then I saw him from the front: forehead gashed open, face swollen and blackened with bruises, jaw rigid. The bone showed through where his nose had split, and his liver where the blade had ruptured it. Neither Luc, nor Bako or I dared to pull out the knife that was buried so deep.

A fly passed, swirling in the air, and settled on the wound, folding its black wings. I saw its tiny head and thin legs go right inside, then it flew off, red with bubbles of blood which began to gush around the knife. In the solitude of the room, we were divided from the world of the living, stricken by more than fear – by a horror both atrocious and solemn. So death wasn't just a word. It was spread out here before my eyes, and I couldn't turn away. I sat down for a moment on a divan, to catch my breath in the subdued intimacy of the lamplight, sinking into warm, deep cushions. I felt as if I was an important guest who had been left there, glass in hand, forgotten by the master of the house.

In the middle of the room, stretched out on the rug in a pool of blood, the body went on emptying itself in jerky spasms. Like the slimy trails snails leave behind, reddish saliva oozed from the corners of his mouth, rolled along his chin and down his neck. The man vomited up his soul. The blood began to flow as from the side of a still-warm beast. In a religious silence, a clock beat steady seconds. We could hear the wind blowing outside. There was a hollow in my gut. I felt a wave of nausea and disgust travel from my head down to my legs. I watched Bako, who stood transfixed in hypnotic stillness, his face very pale. Luc wiped his sweaty brow, his face ravaged by panic and nervous twitches. The fly struggled to find a way out, knocking against the window panes. It too was floating in this strange, porous universe, in the gloomy confines where the solemn hand of destiny had shown itself. With feverish fingers, Bako lit a cigarette. We were alone with death. The cat on the piano miaowed and we all jumped. Shaking with anguish, Luc stepped forward; the cat disappeared over the balcony.

In the mirror above the fireplace, by the light of the night that filtered through the half-drawn curtains, I saw my face petrified with terror. The cold went right through my back. I felt a sharp pain in my neck. My gaze met the dead man's; beneath his reddish-blue, cold eyelids, his fish eyes stared at me through viscous liquid. His demise, heralding my own, ensured the worst possible fate lay in store for me. The lips of the corpse seemed to smile at me ironically, as if he knew his death would kill our lives. Most of the objects in the room now looked purely decorative in view of the climax of the scene that was being played out. I was the attentive theatre-goer, watching the play of his own life. The moonlight slipped a bluish shadow through the shutters. We heard a dog bark outside, it vibrated for a long time. There was a bad smell in the air. Death wasn't just a word, then, but this purple liquid flowing from a pierced chest.

At the end of that scene, I'd have so liked him to get to his feet slowly, that actor, under the beaming lights, for him to bow to the crowd as he had the night before, in his costume of silver armour. I felt the whole weight of the sky on my skull, a shovelful of earth falling on my face like my own ashes in the night of time. The spirit of the dead man was present, permeating the room. Then I threw myself at his rigid form and strangled him with my bare hands. I could feel his Adam's apple roll between my fingers. I couldn't loosen my grip, I banged his head on the ground and wept. It was Luc who gently picked me up.

'Hey . . . hey . . . come on . . . It's over now.'

Before we went down the stone staircase to get Sikko, Luc took an overcoat from the wardrobe and laid it delicately over the bloody corpse. He did it the way you might drape a shawl over your girlfriend's shoulders, like a man bending over to pray at a deathbed. At last, we stepped over the still, cold shape and went downstairs. Veiled in shadows, the night had slipped from under our feet into a dawn of murderers.

My head was filled with shooting stars. Now I knew how things come and go: unexpected, violent, swift, in a lightning flash, life spurts out in the slitting of a throat. Light and shadow. The majestic motion of the setting sun.

Luc signalled to Sikko that we had to get out fast. Before we left, we gagged all the people and tied them to each other.

We followed the same road back that we had come on. As a blind man watches the sunrise, batting his eyelids, we emerged from the depths. Our breathing became less troubled. The fresh air of dawn suddenly revived us. Here, there and everywhere, millions of people were waking up; men, women and children, who didn't kill. Luc kept repeating the story to Sikko, who nodded his head and tapped the steering wheel with the palm of his right hand.

On the way back, so few other cars overtook us you'd have thought the roads were empty. Le Vésinet, Rueil, Nanterre, Puteaux, the whole trip passed me by. I'd have trouble describing it. I tried helplessly to remember the moment when it had all gone wrong, replaying the scene in my head a thousand times as if to hold on to it. Driving along like this, at daybreak, I felt it was all a bad dream and I was about to wake up. All the tension stored up from the night before was suddenly released in an uncontrollable fit of laughter that overwhelmed Bako, moving on to Luc and Sikko and then me; an endless stream of laughter swelled our chests, took flight, crossed the skies, swirled in the dawn and echoed in the distance behind us.

At Macadam Squat we were dazzled when Sikko, bare-chested, emptied the bag stuffed with rubies, emeralds, diamonds, rings, precious gold necklaces and strings of pearls onto the bed. In the dark room, the jewels glistened with light. It might have been pirates' treasure excavated from an underwater grotto, a heavy black wooden coffer studded with starfish, crammed with gold and precious stones, still streaming with seaweed. The night's plunder, piled up in a heap on the bedcovers, gleamed strangely. From the end of the gold chains, a chorus of soft tick-ticking filled our ears.

Luc scooped up a fistful of jewels, felt their weight and let them pour through his fingers; there was a clinking sound, he looked like he was enjoying himself. He nodded sagely.

'We should wrap them in tissue paper,' he suggested. He put each object carefully back in the bag. For a long while we sat there contemplating our booty. My thoughts were spinning: the jewels, rings, watches, money, all these riches that danced before my eyes were like a sky full of restless stars. I sat there staring at them, eyes open wide, convinced that in their own mute way the fiery sparks that intermittently shot out were trying to tell me something. For a moment I was afraid. I saw the stabbed man lying in the room, his inflated shadow was projected on the wall opposite me; I felt linked to it by some obscure bond. I closed my eyes for a second, they were heavy with exhaustion, and my whole head ached. Sikko fingered the banknotes, crumpled them, put a wad to his nose and, holding it by the tips of his fingers, sniffed hard. He inhaled with giddy pleasure.

'Money has no smell,' he pronounced with a malicious laugh and adolescent abandon. We split the cash equally, until we could sell the jewels, statuettes and books. We all agreed to steer clear of each other and lie low for a while. It was better for everyone if no one saw us together. Bako and I left with the canvas bag. I'd stuffed it with banknotes and a few carefully chosen objects.

Rue Saint-Denis had a reputation for being a neighbourhood of cut-throats, thieves, prostitutes, crooks and gamblers. It drew as many young provincials visiting the big city as tourists from abroad, who walked the pavements with great care, especially at night. In the days of Saint Louis, the Convent for the Daughters of God had been built as a refuge for reformed prostitutes and fallen women, sinners who'd abused their bodies all their lives before sinking into begging. We lived in a room on the third floor of a building there – number 175 to be precise. A friend of Bako's, Jean-François, had rented us the place while he was away in Valence. The furniture comprised a chair and a dull wooden wardrobe. The bed wasn't made and hadn't been for days. The stove had two hobs, both piled high with dirty saucepans; the milk in one of them was growing a pale skin of mould.

Bako would stretch out on the bed, fully clothed, and go to sleep like that, gasping for breath. Or he'd lie with a hand behind his neck and an ashtray on the sheet in the tiny bedroom and smoke bad weed. A fly buzzed around his head and the shrieks of children echoed from school playgrounds. Since our return, he'd succumbed to resentment and fever. Every night he drifted between a half-waking stupor and a light, sweat-soaked sleep. Six days went by like this in total inertia. Sometimes he'd wake with a start, panting, and sit on the edge of the bed to wait till his heart stopped pounding. His clothes were strewn all over the floor, carelessly rolled up in balls; mine were slung over the back of a chair. A strip light glared at walls papered with pink and green flowers. Night and day the room was drowned in the din from the street, with its perpetual round of drunks, fraudsters and playful slang. Next to Bako, on the bedside table, the radio was switched on and music poured out, interrupted every half-hour by a newsflash that we would listen to avidly.

We had been cooped up in this room for over a week now. We spent whole days lying around in a fetid stink of sweat and tobacco. Every second brought us inexorably closer to the police; the storm brewing in the outside world hung over our heads. The city became suffocating. Outside, the sun scorched the street, so hot it melted the tarmac, which stuck to people's shoes. And so it was, every day. The heat wouldn't let up. I could hardly breathe. The air was so heavy it weighed on your chest. It was impossible to sleep now. I would get up and walk round the room noiselessly, like a sleepwalker. The ear can only make out sounds and voices at night, when pain and dreams resonate like footsteps. You can even hear the echo of your own heartbeat. My stomach was knotted with dread. We heard the tramping of feet and people jostling under the street lights, and every so often the sound of a chase; whistles blowing followed by a stampede. As yet there was nothing to do but wait. We felt we were being watched. Everywhere we saw eyes spying on us, in bars, windows, walls; faces, people, thousands of mouths that murmured as we went by, 'It's them . . . it's them . . .', a thousand index-fingers pointing at us. A passer-by had only to smile and, once at the end of the street, we'd break into a run. We'd spend our days in the room sitting on the bed or lying down, lighting one cigarette after another. We'd blow the smoke at the ceiling and watch as it curled upwards. Or we'd pace up and down, round and round like dazed monkeys.

We'd only go out in the gaudy night, to eat, standing up in the tiny Greek café, hidden in the recess of a wall. The aroma of grilled lamb, greasy chips and merguez sausages cooked in the open wafted over to the wide-open porches where, hidden in the grey half-light, starving tramps slept, their tongues damp and sour. When we got back, we'd throw ourselves on the bed, which still wasn't made. I drifted between sleep and wakefulness. I'd jerk myself awake, prey to the craziest fears. My nerves were so taut that my brain threatened to burst through my skull.

Sometimes I thought I was back with that motionless shape in Saint-Germain-en-Laye, as if the man's body had joined mine, enveloping me. I poured myself into his remains; my veins swelled with his blood. Life drained out of me. Death took over. His guts, flesh and organs breathed through my nostrils. The smell of his meat floated in the tiny room, carried away by the evening wind. The cutting edge of the sharp blade, the blue of the steel, appeared through waves of nausea. The act of killing kept repeating. His fragile head still hung from the end of his neck, beneath his thick hair. During the day, I no longer knew whether we'd lived or dreamed the whole tragedy. An unspeakable disgust overwhelmed me. I was tied, alive, to a corpse. A smell of rich earth and rotten flowers emanated from the floorboards. I was suffocating. The dead man hovered between the walls. On the morning of the fifteenth day, at the newspaper kiosk on the corner, between the small print and the headlines, a story down one side divided by a photograph caught my eye. The dead man's face was there in a morning edition, multiplied by the printing presses.

'Mr Jean-Baptiste Tibon, aged fifty-five, a lawyer by profession, has been found dead. The ongoing inquiry points to murder. The crime squad are following leads. Mr Tibon was apparently surprised during a weekend at his home in the country. He was a respected member of the Saint-Germain-en-Laye community. The circumstances of the crime remain unclear.'

The sky was covered by a vault of black clouds; a bad omen. A slow-brewing storm hung heavy over the city. The August heat hugged the ground, crawling like a snake. Since the newspaper's publication, we'd shut ourselves in the small room, pacing up and down, chain-smoking. Life became unbreathable. Now we knew that the inquiry, proceeding by cross-checking, juxtaposition and collating a slow accumulation of facts, would lead overwhelmingly to us, the clues falling perfectly into place since our last escapade. Already there were furtive comings and goings of cars. Uniformed policemen, lurking at the corner of rue Saint-Denis and Étienne-Marcel metro station, had been carrying out checks on every passer-by for three days now. All roads to the city centre had been blocked. The local papers, in their 'In Brief' columns, had also printed the victim's photograph with the caption: 'Mr Tibon, lawyer, found murdered in his villa. The police are pursuing their inquiries.' The uprightness of his life was mentioned, too. For as long as the hunt went on, we read all the press, hoping to find answers to our questions. But no, there were just the usual stories about plane crashes, bombarded cities, capital cities being occupied, dead children, enough to make the ink leak from your fingers.

The only window in the room opened onto the street.

Bako sneaked a glance. A police car drove by, its shrill siren screeching up at us. They were looking for us everywhere. Bako lit a cigarette and waited, on edge, for the siren to fade in the distance. I watched him drag himself to the bed and immediately fall asleep. Me, I couldn't even doze, I just tossed and turned in anguish next to him, trying to think. On the night of the thirtieth day, impatient bangs at the door roused us abruptly from our sleep.

'Who is it?' We'd kept the door permanently locked.

'Crime squad and juvenile squad. Open up.'

We were still drowsy, but I automatically scanned the room for anything that might compromise us. Bako was so terrified he was trembling all over.

They knocked again.

'Open this door or we'll break it down.'

Pulling up our trousers over our hips, we unlocked the door. They burst in violently, revolvers in hand.

'You're under arrest. Hands up.'

We did as we were told. They approached us slowly. We put up our hands higher. They went through our pockets, turned the room upside down. They seemed irritated to find nothing on us. The room was full of armed policemen watching us intently, their faces hard and wary. We kept our arms in the air, facing the wall. Saliva dried in my throat. Escape was impossible; the window was just a tiny hole. Beneath the crumpled blanket pulled to one side of the bed, the policemen searched for things; certainly the crime weapon. They found only the rings and watches that we still had left and a few francs scattered on the floor.

From that day on, all the dark prophecies of my childhood flashed through my life. I was only just thirteen and already an accomplice to murder, and I didn't even have the strength of an assassin. They handcuffed our hands behind our backs. Stunned, I walked down the stairs, making every step creak. It was like walking to the scaffold. My legs felt very heavy. The cops held us firmly by the arms. They carried their revolvers at their hips, hands resting on them, ready to draw at the first sign of a struggle. Down we went, our bodies sweating with fear in the stifling heat, so intense it even scaled the shaky banister. We crossed the little blind alley. The stench of the filth and rubbish that spilled from the bins piled by the gutter was suffocating on this summer night.

That stormy damp of Paris. There was nothing you could do. It even seeped inside houses through half-open windows. There was no air in this furnace. Idlers in shirtsleeves strolled the pavements, endlessly coming and going. Others lingered on café terraces, where glasses were set out on tables. Cars rolled by, headlights dimmed or dipped, trying to get through the crowds that spilled onto the street. Along the walkways of apartment blocks, leaning in doorways, half-naked prostitutes fanned themselves with their hands like Spanish dancers. You could sometimes hear them snarling insults and obscenities which even the drunks who frequented the local bars had never heard. It was here that, one evening, I saw two women rolling on the pavement, shouting and spitting, pulling out fistfuls of hair in the middle of the street which roars, howls and bellows. There were the regulars, too, loyal punters who'd been coming here for years. Well-bred people always wind up in disreputable places at least once; the squalor excites their sick curiosity.

A woman gave me the once-over. She put her lipstick back in her bag and brought out a powder compact just as we passed. From one end of the street to the other, gangs of boys in town from the suburbs talked to each other as they beeped their horns. They had their girlfriends with them, who chatted just as loudly and leaned over the car doors to catch a glimpse of the tarts. They shrieked with hysterical laughter amid the noise of wheels and engines. Using a pocket mirror, a prostitute touched up her make-up, a lick of the tongue and her mouth was as good as new, a dab of mascara followed by a fine layer of powder. Finally she gave her fringe a quick brush, pulled at her dress to unstick it from her sweaty skin and fanned herself for the benefit of the voyeurs who came and went from one bar to the next. The sun's rays, trapped all day long on car roofs and bodywork, fanned out into the night. Engines throbbed, spitting scarves of exhaust fumes pungent with burnt petrol. The kids had their radios on full blast, windows down. Sex shop signs flashed. It was night-time in rue Saint-Denis, with its thousand artificial lights. The movement of this seething crowd was familiar to me. The drunks belched into the air.

The police cars' blue lights rotated like helicopter blades, sweeping the darkness with their red and blue beams. Alerted by the first radio message, several cars were patrolling the streets. Our descriptions had been circulated. The neighbourhood was sealed off on all sides. We would never have been able to escape. Uniformed and plainclothes police poured out of police vans. The crime squad and the juvenile squad were collaborating on this case. We'd been identified from the very first witness statements. It was our youth which had proved fatal. The police van's siren could be heard a mile off. When it pulled up, loiterers just thought it was another brawl. Patrol cars, their doors open, blocked the entrance to the building. Already, rubbernecks were gathering. Police vans wove through, engines roaring. A cop cleared a path for us through the crowd, pushing aside the people in the way.

'Come on, stand back now. Back, everyone. Come on, make way. There's nothing to see. Let them through.'

The crowd closed around us. Another policeman, powerfully built, went ahead to clear access to the van. Shouts went up here and there. A few reporters were already on the scene, carrying heavy Nagra tape recorders. We were hardly out in the open before the photographers aimed their flashes at our faces. Amid the hysterical clicking of cameras we crossed the dead end, pale-faced, blinded and blinking. For the last time, I heard the noise of the street die away. Four cars were parked along the pavement. We were shoved onto the back seat. A policeman got in on either side of us. Another slid behind the wheel and started the engine. We drove off at top speed, siren wailing, with a second van right behind.

I thought the police would find reasons to hate us and rough us up to make us confess to the murder. It turned out quite differently. When we arrived, they removed our handcuffs and put us in separate cells. The juvenile squad inspectors seemed almost glad to have us back on the premises. Over time, a kind of obscure complicity had developed between us. A murder inquiry sharpened their wits. In the end, they'd grown weary of our muggings, indifferent to our breaking and entering. They were bored. But now they were grateful to us for reawakening the hunter's instinct that lay dormant within them. Tired of our small-time pilfering, they were suddenly all ears; it was as if they agreed to look at us for the first time. I saw a flicker of humanity in their eyes, almost a kindly look; the sacrament of murder raised us to the rank of child prodigies. Death clothed us in its regal splendour. It was as if the crime was itself a glorious achievement. But was it us or the dead man who inspired this respectful admiration?

We were each questioned, not without a certain deference, the kind a major suspect might claim when faced with representatives of the law. I wasn't used to the style of questioning practised at the higher levels. There was a sort of ceremonial emphasis in their attitude, a degree of consideration shown only to important criminals.

This formality made a change from the mocking familiarity of the old days, and the joyful mood of the inner city police stations when we were tied to the radiators with safety belts amid insults and throaty laughter. We'd been arrested more than once and beaten up mercilessly even more often. Frowning, an inspector read out the arrest report, a cigarette stuck to the corner of his mouth, his head tilted back. He scrutinised me at every comma, through narrowed eyes. When he'd completed his rather long reading, I understood the weight of the charges brought against me. But the overall meaning of the document was a total mystery, the form and content seemed so confused. One of the police officers offered me a cigarette; my chest swelled slightly, from vanity. This gesture honoured me and I was happy to join in a game of cops and robbers. Like a big-screen bandit, I lit the cigarette with a virile flourish. I felt a strange sense of unreality; these policemen were here to serve me now.

The inspector gave me another hard, inquisitive stare, and tapped his fingers on the desk.

'You have nothing else to confess?'

'No!'

'Fine. As you like.'

He pulled some crime scene photos from a briefcase, along with some glossy enlargements. He spread them out on the table.

'I suppose you recognise this man,' he said, both hands resting on the file. 'Your fingerprints were found on his neck. Everything points to your guilt. We have all the proof we need, we have the crime weapon and various witnesses who are ready to testify. We even found a trace of the blade on the bone, here,' said the inspector, looking impatient. 'So it's pointless to deny it.'

Since our arrest, Bako and I had been kept apart during the interrogation sessions. Confronted with this much irrefutable evidence, there was nothing I could do. My reaction was extreme: I felt myself flush, I swallowed my spit.

'I repeat, think about it . . . Your friend risks the death

penalty and you're looking at a life sentence. He'll be charged with a premeditated crime to which you're the accomplice, don't forget. I wouldn't get your hopes up as to the final sentence,' he added, 'but if you give me the names of your accomplices, I promise to speak up for you with the judges.'

The reality of prison hit me. My mouth was dry, my throat squeezed tight till it hurt. The police officer urged me to speak fearlessly and assured me that he'd personally see to it that my and Bako's prison terms were reduced.

'Trust me,' he said.

I gave him the names and addresses of our accomplices, but the strange thing was, I felt no remorse. The soft voice of my interrogator had the mysterious, invisible charm of a priest hearing your confession in the dark. I almost enjoyed my declarations. I quietly listed the places Luc and Sikko usually hung out. I heard myself give a full confession, leaving out no detail of my guilt. A faintly sarcastic smile momentarily lit up the inspector's face.

'You see? It's not so hard to shop your friends. Now I'll have a word with the judge on your behalf so you'll be sentenced fairly and favourably,' he promised.

I learned later that it was on the basis of my confession that the prosecutor in the trial was able to establish that the murder had not been premeditated. Betrayal had been born. Later I would learn how to betray others even better, and myself, to sell my soul if necessary, the better to forget. I've always been capable of committing any crime to save my skin. Something evil ruled my life and grew stronger as I got older. I don't know if I chose it, but this condition swiftly thrust itself upon me. The way I'd imagined myself to be was what I had now become. At that moment I was afraid of myself, of the toxic decay that welled up in me, an essence of shit, flesh and slime. I know people need heroes, but I had never seen any trace of hero worship in myself.

The mirror in that office reflected back to me the first shocking revelation of my life: my cowardice. I thought of the others, the ones who would say they'd always known I'd come to no good and that the die had been cast long ago. Much later I found out that in his statement Bako had confessed to every action and event leading up to the crime, but refused to collaborate with the police when it came to squealing on his friends. Throughout the interrogations he'd shown true loyalty, giving only trivial information, having already confessed that he was the murderer. Only one thing separated us: a sense of dignity. I have to admit my confessions of guilt were obtained by honest means and no force was used in that stifling crime squad office where, under the harsh lights, I answered their questions. The clues to the evening's events were mercilessly listed on those records, marked with my fingerprints.

The inspector slipped a form into the typewriter and wound it round with a creak. Then he looked up and said: 'I'm listening.' His eyes bored into me. The evidence was piled up on his desk.

The sharp, rapid patter of the typewriter keys vibrated between my temples. He asked me more questions and I had to give detailed replies. He wouldn't accept any evasion. The monotonous clicking of his typewriter echoed in my brain. For the first time my life was classified, delivered up before my eyes. Everything I was was sealed in those words. He tapped away on the old machine and I watched, fascinated. I saw my reality being put into words. During my deposition, I began to think of the whole history of this ill-fated breed, written up on headed police notepaper. I thought of all those tumultuous lives lying on registers in administrative archives, like unfinished works scattered through the magistracy's basements, all those sad confessions consigned to the tomes of the powers-that-be, and of my own, in print, that would suffer the same fate. I could have read my own destiny in any one of those stories, which are inscribed nowhere else. From fathers to sons, they were all there. I was welcomed among them. Blood ties between the dead were gradually renewed. They greeted me with open arms like travellers who recognise each other on a platform. Their history was buried by the centuries; there were no words to say it nor ink to write it. They were people from another world who seemed to sleep at the bottom of damp cellars, their faces flecked in shadow.

Later, a grey-suited man arrived: the examining magistrate. He held out a piece of paper which I signed, murmuring: 'Yes, sir, yes, sir,' without even reading it. I was exhausted. The next morning, a police van took me to Savigny-sur-Orge. They kept Bako longer, trying to extract more information. Our arrest was headline news. The journalists reported events under the title 'Baby-faced Killers'. They turned our lives into pulp fiction to throw to a crowd that bayed for monsters, heroes and victims. The publication of our ages, though our names weren't revealed, added to the frenzy. I read various details about myself with some surprise. Our arrest was interpreted in different ways. Some ascribed to us a sort of precocious machiavellianism, but they didn't want to hear the rest of the story, it didn't matter to them. No one would ever know about the sleazy goings-on in that house, not the press, nor the judge, nor the public. An order was given – who knows where from? – to the effect that nothing but the crime should be revealed. And so it was. The reporters' versions varied slightly and inevitably contradicted each other according to whether they were left or right wing: for some we were criminals, for others, martyrs. Both were wrong, of course, as usual. Very little really separates the thief from the honest man, absurdly little. The arrest of the pettiest thief salves the good conscience of human beings, as if condemning him proves their own innocence. The facts as reported were strangely inaccurate. But who cared, as long as the words were the kind to fire the imagination? The press doggedly set about inflaming public opinion to fever pitch.

Outside the walls, a pale sun shone, people passed by and occasionally a peal of laughter or the rev of a car reached me. Sometimes, in the evening, as I lit a cigarette and turned thoughts over and over in my mind, hands clutching the bars, I'd watch without blinking as a corner of the sky went red, then violet, until the last rays filled the streets with twilight. Part of me tried to remember the world I had left. In the distance I'd hear the hum of life and my eyes filled with tears. The days were just one long rumination, monotonous like the sly chatter of the warders.

I was banged up in Savigny-sur-Orge, a renowned borstal. The idea was to straighten out wayward young adolescents, like trees born twisted on the edge of a cliff. It was serious forestry work. 'Saplings need to be staked,' the young offenders' judge commented in passing. The childhood of all these poor wretches, shoved around, shunted and beaten, all thrown together in shared cells like skeletons in a ditch, washed up in this place. Only in borstal can you weigh out night and day, as though at each end of a see-saw with you in the middle. Sometimes it is a man and dust that are weighed. The sky is filled with the kind of haze that light can't pierce. Thousands of kids had already stood here on their own two feet, before falling, swept away by gusts of air into the formless mass of experience. From the mouths of fathers to the breath of sons, the murmur of sorrow is taken up time and again. Grief is catching, just like happiness.

The screw was obese and hostile. Hoisting up his stomach, which spilled over his belt, he said:

'Your name's Tarik Hadjaj, isn't it?'

'Yes,' I answered, surprised. But after all, it could be possible the warder had always known my name. He stared at me a long while, like a snake facing its prey. His face was hard, square and dour. A wisp of moustache adorned his upper lip. A dull grunt accompanied every word he uttered. Papers, prints, photos, committal procedures, emptying pockets, confiscation of all valuable objects in exchange for an ID number. Finally, the locker room. I was ordered to undress, which I did. Under the watchful eye of the warders, I awkwardly pulled off my clothes, turning to face the wall. I needed a good minute or two to get them all off.

Finally, naked from head to toe, I slowly turned towards them.

'Bend over.'

I obeyed. It was the regulation search: open your mouth, cough, raise your tongue, cough, lean forward, cough, legs apart. Then out you go, with your blanket, bowl and grey uniform of rough cloth. The warder pushed me ahead of him down a long corridor. Each door opened onto another door which opened onto a wall among other walls, solid and impossible to climb.

'In here,' he said. With the blanket folded in my hands, the screw shoved me into a small individual cell. So that I wouldn't be a bad influence on the other inmates, they'd put me in isolation. Each inmates' wing bore the name of a French province: Brittany, Alsace, Lorraine, Poitou, etc. Iron bed and shelf fixed to the wall, wooden chair and table screwed to the floor. I went into that cell as if into an overcoat of stone. It was still full of the life of the inmate who'd only just left. I could smell his soul in the mould that filled my throat. I tried not to breathe. The pungent odour of sweat mixed with tobacco and spunk made me feel sick.

On the walls where shadow theatres played at night, yet other boys had exhausted their fantasies of rare sensual delights, their wrists simulating the caresses of queens with gold bracelets round their arms, perfumed and adorned for them alone. Of course the beds creak rhythmically under the weight of solitude. I've known that desire which is just a painful shiver down the spine. You had to rid yourself of the intimate secret which escapes through your penis, the pressure slowly pulsating in the blood to a shudder. We've never moved on from our mothers' white, damp inner thighs.

The only female smells came from the nurses. Mademoiselle Karina came back to haunt me. My senses were numbed by my fantasies. A bitter pleasure stirred in my belly, especially in summer, when I'd lie naked on my blanket in the oppressive heat. You'd almost have given yourself to your own shadow. In the women's wing, hysterical inmates would undo their blouses and rub themselves against the walls. I had never yet held a girl in my arms.

Over the years, I'd compiled a picture book using photos from porn mags. On fine days, through the barred windows we'd watch girls pass by who, without knowing it, would bounce daylight into our eyes. Their brightness shrouded our shadows in a swarm of summer midges. Just seeing them made our cocks stiffen under the flimsy trouser fabric. We'd glimpse their legs parting as they walked. At night we'd carry them all off into the thick, wet darkness. I didn't have the patience to wait for mine to get free of her jumble of underskirts. I took her in the soft rustle of a ripped skirt. For sure, the walls absorbed our dreams. Once you came back from there, you were completely different from those who'd never been. Did another life exist where young people could imagine the future and, much later, remember the past? Without it being in any way decided for them? There'll always be something to say about the life of one of those kids with bright eyes, a slender waist and a gentle, handsome round face; something unsaid between heaven and earth.

A naive drawing of a cat woman with a pussy of thick golden hair covered the wall. The caption engraved beneath it: 'The cat's got my tongue.' I thought about the hands that had fashioned this erotic drawing. It was primitive, like the black ink tattoos that adorned the young inmates' bodies. Written desires punctuated their flesh, entwined, squeezed, mingling with the cement. Graffiti introduced me to the traces of men stuck in the shadow of ruins, the marks they made were barely visible cave drawings, beneath the clay, in the grey earth of the centuries. Scribbles made by children's hands smudged with ink or chalk, badly carved words that form the blue sky at the edge of the walls. To bend one's destiny to the arc of hieroglyphs dug deep into the plaster, or gash the flesh, leaving furrows like the tracks of chariot wheels in the mud. More deprived than a caveman, to scratch with a rusty nail a sign among the other signs, leaving an imprint of grief for the stranger who will come one day in his turn to rot in this hole, so that he'll know he is not alone. The trembling of that hand is accompanied by the millennia. This mark of the misfit tells the next boy who doesn't understand that he is like us, which otherwise he'd never realise. This trace lives on in the wall, bearing the conscience of all those who have passed through here. Just as, on the day you enter the coffin, a tombstone is engraved, among the fraternity of the dead. Poor brothers of the shadows.

At the start of my imprisonment the narrowness of the cell didn't bother me. I'd only leave it briefly for exercise. Later, in the mornings, I felt I was waking up in a space that had mysteriously shrunk while I was asleep. A month went by like that, then another, and then years piled onto the hours and the days. Dawn always added its own pain to the night. The sand trickled away in the cumulative silence. In my cell, I had time to reflect on the events that had brought me there. Under the mattress I discovered the heroes of those small cartoon-strip magazines: Blek le Roc, Akim, Rodéo – a whole library from the cheap market stalls was there, in those images with the colours of childhood. Sitting on the chair or lying on the bed, I read them to help me pass the time. The warders' heavy steps echoed to the end of the corridor.

In the yard, a group of boys ambled over casually. They gave me the once-over and whispered together. I leaned against the wall, trying to hide my embarrassment.

'You, where you from?' asked one, point-blank.

'Nanterre,' I answered.

They were boys from the same background as me, dressed in the grey cotton uniform. At first, everyone treated me with hostility and suspicion. Like a stray dog in the street, I had to show my teeth to disguise my fear. We watched each other. They were sizing me up. As yet we knew each other only vaguely. You had to prove to yourself how hard you were, no tears or moaning allowed. But gradually they started to smile at me when they saw me come into the yard. There was no solidarity between us. We survived in small gangs, each in his respective tribe, making the usual compromises, and as for snitching . . .

All those boys were familiar to me; we were twigs off the same tree. I heard in their voices the accents of my old friends, who I'd meet astride their motorcycles on street corners in rough neighbourhoods. I recognised them by a look in their eyes I alone could detect. I saw my own likeness in a glance, a way of walking. Without knowing them, I knew all their moves. They weren't surprised by mine. Each inmate seemed to have nothing in common with the ones before, yet all had the same origins. None of us was different from the others in any way. Their secrets was mine. I remembered every face I came across, as if from another existence. My life did nothing but gaze at itself in a kind of narcissistic mirror.

In the corridors, we'd swap dirty jokes over and over again, about voracious lovers, duped husbands or wily crooks conning each other. We told each other a whole load of things that had never even happened. Our lives became entangled; they were so alike that we carried on with daily life vicariously, living in one person's dreams and dying in another's, leaving our destinies undisturbed. Even the lines on our hands looked identical.

The days assumed other dimensions. They were no longer just the mechanical timeless state suggested by the absurd tick-tock of a thousand clocks, none of which told the time. I listened to the silence. I could only hear the sound of the screws pacing the corridor. It was impossible to sleep. When dawn came, a ray of sun sometimes shimmered on the dusty bars. Sitting on the bed, I listened to the lifeblood drain from days that slipped by slowly. How can I describe to you a blind wait in full sunlight? Prison taught me the patience needed to die each night. You sleep with your eyes open, you piss, you shit, and none of it matters any more. Life had no meaning for me now.

Each of us killed the dead time whatever way he could, clinging to the calendar, crossing off the days, underlining holidays. At Christmas and New Year, besides the special meal they put on, the canteen was decorated with paper garlands, some of which fell down. A group of warders picked them up with the help of inmates. The others hung off the walls, as pathetic as flowers at dead men's feet. The cell windows were very narrow, not just obstructed but covered by wire mesh. I watched the town and heard voices through the grille. I could see illuminated windows which to me looked further away than the stars in the sky. Time trickled by, with its brawls and its intrigues, with the boring deals we made with the warders who monitored us.

We spent our days yelling the rudest things we could think of, to prove our virility in front of the others. Curses, complaints and groans. You couldn't speak frankly to anyone. I was not at peace, either with myself or with the other kids, who I thought had that violent, dangerous look about them. In prison, hatred is the only thing that lasts; time patinates it like a statue. At night, no flesh compares to your own. We caressed our curves as if they were made of bronze.

I dreamed of breaking out. I intended to use any possible means of escape. I devised various plans. Over the weeks, I shaped a makeshift key with which to pick the lock of the cell. Late at night, when all you could hear were snores and coughing fits, and the whole prison was plunged in gloom, I would sharpen its teeth on the cement floor. Its accuracy improved every day. I already saw myself in the city, behind a steering wheel, escaping in a cloud of dust.

Alas, in the first year of my imprisonment, during a cell inspection, the warders found my lucky key under the mattress. No sooner discovered than a fist landed between my eyes. I fell backwards. One of the screws kept coming at me, as the other watched. I saw hatred in his hard stare. My mouth tasted of salty blood. Abuse poured down on my head. My attempt at escape earned me twenty days' solitary in an old, evil-smelling cell. No ventilation at all. The stench made me ill. I couldn't even take a shower. I had no idea how long I'd been wearing the same clothes.

Insects kept invading the sweaty plank I lay on, or flitted around the light that was kept on permanently. That hole had been rotting away for more than a century. The summer heat permeated the stone and iron. I walked barefoot round and round the cell. I muttered to myself in a monotone. It was there I developed the bad habit of talking to myself out loud. With my head on the old pillow, I'd plunge into my long dreams of peaceful constellations, silently seeking the star that had to be shining for me somewhere. I flew very high, setting off in the light years between heaven and earth, into the cosmos with its comets, miracles and prodigies, amid the leaps and somersaults of the stars. I was small enough to enter this immense universe. I was gone with the winds, the cyclones and planets, the ring of Saturn, Gemini, Jupiter, Uranus, Mars. I whispered my secrets to God as my soul surged towards the light. I myself was part of the sky. I passed through walls, over the roofs of Savigny. I escaped in a lyrical flight from the lowest depths into the skies, just to catch a glimpse of infinity and breathe a little air. I'd gladly have landed on the last star that trembled at the zenith, a vagabond among Venus, Orion, Betelgeuse, blinking in the dizzying galaxy, and disappearing in stardust from the Triangle to Sagittarius. My eyesight was ruined on that plaster ceiling with its grey hanging light bulb.

In a way it seemed to me that I was luckier than the other inmates, because at least I had no one to bemoan the paths I'd strayed onto. On visiting days, from first light, families would turn up and settle down to wait by the prison entrance, ranged along the wall. The queue formed in the cold, in snow or rain. The children, who'd come too, stood shivering. So many mothers, sisters, fiancées and brothers waited for their visits. They had to walk through all the gates, past the metal detector.

Voices reached me through the walls as inmates banged on the doors, cursing and crying. I heard the shouts of boys fighting like lunatics, swearing and yelling. I listened till they went quiet. The rush of warders' boots along the corridors. I heard the jangling of keys, doors slamming open and closed.

'One of them hanged himself last night. He ejaculated as he died' was the word in the yard.

Jean-Claude R, nicknamed 'Doe-Eyes' because he had tattoos on either side of his eyelids, ruled over the young offenders like a king. He was a bit older than us and everyone respected him. I knew from hearsay that he was nearly seventeen, but apart from that I knew nothing about him. I'd already noticed him in the canteen – he watched me closely as he ate. His small green eyes were so deep-set his stare was like one big hole. We were enemies from day one. He was tall and heavily built with red hair, a colossus with an angular face and a broken nose, his fists always at the ready. I distrusted his big dumb grin, which he would pull right in your face. More than once I caught him sizing me up from the corner of his eye. All the spirit and energy of this wild young male shone from his crafty eyes. He was challenging me. Every street kid knew how important these brawls were; every new inmate had to undergo this kind of test. Doe-Eyes was looking forward to what would follow with malicious pleasure. To fall out with him would make you a gang of enemies.

The showers provided a flimsy shelter for soulless embraces, a dodgy meeting-place that facilitated all manner of approaches and dark encounters, an initiation to the worst of fates. Little by little, certain boys had got used to yielding indifferently to the insistent caresses of hands in the shadows. Under the gushing water, Doe-Eyes watched me with sly nonchalance. I intrigued him, that much was clear. I saw his eyes shining with sinister, ambiguous desire. I felt the same revulsion as I would for a reptile. His body looked scaly and glazed. And I was horrified by the insidious friendships that were born in this place. First I saw his profile, then he looked me up and down. Finally he turned to face me, staring me in the eye as he soaped his face, neck and torso, before sliding the soap onto his hips, thighs and arse, ending with his genitals. Water streamed over his belly. He stretched out his arm to soap his inner thigh insistently. His hand brushed against his cock, which instantly stiffened. I gave him a violent look, the hardest stare I could muster, but he didn't blink. Making a show of his virility was part of his ritual as gang leader. He always went for the youngest among us. Now he was smiling at me as he washed himself, seeking my collusion. I spat on the floor. He sniggered and showed me a gob of milky phlegm between his teeth; he spat in the palm of his right hand and smeared it along his erect cock. Taunting me, he spat again on his thick, short fingers, turned towards me and performed that tugging motion, up and down. A shower of obscenities poured from his mouth as he slapped his cock with the back of his hand. He came right in front of me, in a spurt of white foam, like oily poison.

'Take my advice, stay out of my way,' he said, planting himself in front of me, legs apart and arms crossed. Then he left.

That showed me what could happen to an adolescent trapped between these four walls, if he breaks down. I learned quickly not to trust anyone. Rubbing up against the wretched makes you wretched. Everything gets spoiled here. What there remains of virginity saved in the soul is no more to be missed than the sexual kind. We know this but we pretend not to, this sacrifice of frail, virginal children on the altar of prison.

My case was due to be heard in the juvenile court. The day before, the officially appointed lawyer came to visit me again; he asked me to trust him. He assured me I had nothing to fear from the trial, which would take place in camera, and if I followed his advice we'd be fine. I didn't really understand why he said we when it was me we were talking about. He asked me to dress smartly, so that I'd make a good impression in court.

'Incidentally,' he said before he left, 'I have copies of all the newspaper articles about you; do you want to take a look?'

'No, thank you, sir,' I said.

'Call me Maître,' he said, 'that's the usual way to address lawyers. Well now, sleep well tonight, so you're on form tomorrow.'

Of course I had nightmares all night. At dawn, a van came to fetch me and take me to court. Two policemen pushed me, handcuffed, into a small gloomy room. It was stifling. They had kept the windows shut.

I waited. A door creaked in the silence. My lawyer appeared, wearing his robe. He reassured me. The policemen unlocked my handcuffs. They ushered me into the dock. I sat down, flanked by two cops. My throat was dry and my palms were moist. I looked straight ahead, to the top of the wall on my right. I could see a huge painting, the portrait of a woman draped in long red robes. She was determinedly leaning all her weight on a sharp sword. Just below stretched a platform and a long table. The hearing was about to begin. The door would open and I'd see them appear. A bitter taste filled my mouth. Lost in my thoughts, I suddenly heard:

'All rise.'

Everyone surged forwards. One of the policemen shook me.

'Can't you stand?'

'Uh, I didn't realise, sir.'

The hearing was declared open. A detailed reading of the charges followed. I recognised the names and places. But after that, I didn't understand the questions put to my lawyer or to the prosecutor. They were using a language the meaning of which I couldn't understand. The presiding judge announced he would proceed to call the witnesses. The court usher read out the names. They came in one by one, then vanished through a side door, so quickly they might have been ghosts. My interrogation began.

'Defendant, please rise.'

I rose. They had me state my name, then the judge listed the charges. Every two or three sentences, he addressed me.

'Do you recognise these facts . . . ? That is right?'

Each time I answered:

'Yes, your honour.'

It seemed very long to me. What could I say? I just stood there, looking at the judge and nodding my head. There was nothing to hold onto. There I was, exposed to their gaze, waiting for a sign that never came. Then everything got muddled in my head. I was tired and confused. All this coming and going, the enclosed space. I wiped off the sweat that ran down my forehead and face. That was when the judge asked the question that plunged the court into silence.

'Why did you strangle the corpse?'

'Because he was dead.'

The prosecutor leaped from his chair, his eyes fixed on me, his whole body trembling with indignation.

'Well, then!' he exclaimed. 'We will take note of this despicable truth coming from the mouth of a thirteen-year-old, capable of wringing with his own bare hands the last breath from this poor man, without a hint of regret or remorse.'

He looked at me with such triumphant hatred I wanted to cry. There was such force in his dramatic intonation I got scared. He seemed suddenly fearsome in his condemnation of my action. His words were heavy with some kind of irrevocable weight, under which I foundered. I vaguely realised that I couldn't take back any of my actions, though I wanted to cancel them out. I'd have liked to look at the judge and explain why I'd done it, but my eyes stayed riveted to the ceiling. My terror made me lose the power of speech.

'Why did you do it?' The man went on curtly. 'Look at me when I talk to you.'

He stood up in his pulpit. But how could I explain the dismal, endless days and nights that had dragged me to this point, and all those things he'd never know? I'd have had to wind back the hands of time to the second I was born. I stood before him, my spirit pushed to breaking point, trying to assemble the scraps that made up my existence, a thousand memories I desperately wanted to forget. The judge's stare paralysed me. I felt a void open up inside me. I felt myself weaken. My ears began to burn.

My lawyer, a novice, got tangled up in never-ending sentences. In his attempt to describe me and justify my actions, he referred to the temptation of evil that may strike at every innocent heart; he evoked the devil inside us all. He was dribbling and shaking like a man possessed; he excitedly described the children of the gutter and life on the street, the thirst, hunger and prostitution, the damnation of angels fallen from heaven to the lowest depths. He brought up Saint Vincent de Paul, who I'd never heard of. His defence shamed me more than my crime. He got bogged down in crude details I never imagined a lawyer could contemplate. Finally, he asked for an acquittal and the chance for rehabilitation. Giddiness overwhelmed me. Stomach ache. Headache. I couldn't go on. A psychiatric report had been requested by the court. The psychiatrist came. He read his conclusions to the judge, which referred to schizophrenia, neurosis and compulsive lying.

'Tarik Hadjaj has lower than average intelligence. He shows numerous signs of mental confusion and affective disorientation. He has no objective notion of reality and takes refuge in fantasy. His behaviour can be explained by symptoms of emotional retardation due to his inability to develop perspective, which means he has lost the sense of good and evil. He suffers from memory loss and periods of amnesia during which he may commit irrevocable acts with no thought of the consequences. He possesses a kind of animal instinct, in a trance-like state. In my opinion, an expert evaluation is recommended. In addition, he suffers from a pathological inability to form and maintain lasting emotional attachments. He is, ladies and gentlemen, a typical example of what we in psychiatry call a borderline personality disorder.'

Then it was the public prosecutor's turn to speak. During the arraignment, I remained seated.

'What do you have to say in your defence?' the judge inquired.

I stood up, sensing the seriousness of the moment. I tried to think of the right words. I looked at the prosecutor. I wanted some kind of forgiveness, something I'd never experienced. But nothing came. I looked down and kept quiet. That's how it is with silent distress. Yet I'd have given anything at that exact moment for words that persuade. But I knew deep down that my life was something I had no understanding of, and it had been that way since I was born. Suddenly, my stomach churned with fear. As I leaned on the bar for support, I gave in to an intense urge to vomit, and not just a little but until I passed out. There's a kind of fear that heaves the gut, stomach and heart in waves of terror. I threw up. Flux and reflux of mucus, strands of foam and starch. It was disgusting. I was spitting out my insides. Bursting, drowned, covered in saliva, I tried to swallow it back down but I kept retching. No one should ever see you puke up the original fear that trembles inside you like a leaf on a tree. It was then I gained some understanding of human sciences; it was a real anatomy lesson. The two policemen got splattered, one by a bit of fatty meat soaked in juice, the other by curdled sauce. There was a moment of silence. Now everyone there was against me. I'd interrupted the rhythm of those magnificent intoning voices, their game of clever repartee. I'd put an end to their fine gesturing in broad daylight. I'd broken the spell. They were furious.

'Get him out! Good God, get that vomiting fool out of here!' the judge shouted.

The blood rose to my head and a veil fell over my eyes, plunging the room in thick fog. I could still hear the sound of footsteps, then my eyes closed and everything went black. I lost consciousness. I was carried onto the bench in the police van and left there to come to my senses.

They debated the nature of my vices amongst themselves for a long time, then they went deep into my childhood. They found nothing but a void. Two police motorbikes shot away from the court, then one, two, three vehicles, all sirens wailing. I was back on the road to Savigny-sur-Orge. I looked at the cracked cell ceiling and had no idea where I was for nearly half a minute. Eventually I remembered. At fourteen, I suddenly understood ten thousand years of a life I hadn't lived. I had felt the brutal surge of time pass through me as I left that courtroom. Outside, earth had changed its season. I knew my life would be a terrible adventure. There are secrets that you know in your body before your mind can grasp them. The tragedy of the poor can only be played out in real life. I saw what my judges had not forgotten of their culture, and I spent ages wondering what perverse matter they dredged to come up with their sentences. I was sorry I wasn't educated like that prosecutor who had the power to kill me with words whose meaning I didn't even know.

The counsel for the prosecution is a man who only believes in the guilt of his fellow man, never in his grace. Mine had the face of someone on whom life had left no trace. He judged my actions as a poisonous prelude to my nature's true intentions. During the trial, I felt he was burrowing into my eyes to find something he could use. The inevitable verdict could be read in his. What else could I say or do to help him justify his private conviction?

As for the judge, I saw him appear in his white ermine with that inimitable bearing that made him the equal of God. Nature had been kind to him physically. His lofty stature gave him a noble bearing, it came easily to him. He expressed himself with perfect evenness of tone. His powers of persuasion were clear. You felt he was irresistibly drawn to judgment. He practised that surprising function of the gods and his conscience seemed to delight in it. Putting other people on trial was his life. He possessed that mastery that's the prerogative of men who are completely sure of their decrees. He was judge by an accident of birth, just as we'd been born accused. He was born innocent for all eternity and that particular virtue depended on condemning us. For his gentle benevolence, or his more or less distracted attention, I'd have crawled at his feet if necessary; but what forgiveness can you beg from someone who denies or ignores his neighbour, from someone who only admits that you exist in his capacity as magistrate, and who one day, sitting opposite the defendants' bench, with the customary nod of the head, condemns you almost without noticing you?

Everything was against us during the trial, against Bako as much as me. Our protestations were useless. All the witnesses, honourable men and women, swore that nothing untoward had occurred that night. After the fainting episode, I decided not to appear in court any more, inventing various illnesses. The final judgment was delivered over a year later. I was condemned to three years' prison without parole and Bako to six, the last years of which he would serve in an adult prison. The sentence was delivered to me in Savigny.

Life was left outside. I felt I'd been inside for an eternity. In the broken mirror, I saw myself as if from a distance of a thousand miles. In the end, the environment rubs off on you; I was rotting away. Winter was the worst, because of the damp and mould, my skin was saturated with the smell. The long days of idleness weighed on me. I stretched out on the bed, I reflected, brooded over time that gnawed at me, or looked disconsolately at the rooftops through the bars; then I'd sit down again, head in hands, half in a dream: there was nothing else to do.

During the day, I waited for night. At night, I waited for day. Standing at the window, I would sometimes stare at the little town until dawn, its trees and its lawns, in the deep silence of night. It was like an expanse of shadows which momentarily burgeoned with a thousand miraculous crystal lights, a dim ballroom suddenly illuminated by the gleaming radiance of a hundred chandeliers, reflected by mirrors. My gaze wandered over the purplish, dingy houses. In the distance, a snow-covered bell-tower that loomed over the park chimed in the humid air, and I stayed there, bewitched. Bright stars shone like lights in the cloud-filled sky. I watched the moon slip across the bars. Every time a plane passed, I imagined the capital cities, the neighbourhoods, the suburbs, the age-old misery of the world it flew over. Men, beasts, countless things, all flooded my mind. It was so quiet I could hear the sound of my blood. Time accumulated in interrupted scratches on the wall, punctuated by blurry intervals of sleep. The endless days and nights suffused the walls and stones where each inmate huddled up, becoming hardened and impenetrable. Each evening, we had to put our desire to sleep. The only link we have with the realm of the senses becomes that miserable contact between hand and naked flesh; but, by revelling in this disgust, you become more and more shut off from others, if only because of the sadness it causes; the mind strays who knows where, and little by little reality itself escapes. Your vision of the world narrows. Prison permeates you through this intimacy with things, making you one of its walls. You can only survive inside by creating a world of fantasy creatures, but they too can slowly lead to alienation.

A girl stood in the doorway, a dazzling apparition lighting up the dark cell, her hand resting on the neck of a reindeer. Dressed in a flimsy veil that covered her breasts and hips, she slowly advanced into this gloomy hole, which was suddenly decorated by her, taking pleasure in the ripple of silk that caressed her naked body. I contemplated her. Her astral beauty slowly wound its way into me. She had a pretty face, framed by blond hair that waved gracefully about her forehead, and big bright eyes. She smiled at me. Her half-open lips gave a glimpse of perfect teeth.

Each evening, I waited for her to materialise, but I never knew if she'd come down from heaven or risen up from the bowels of the earth. She filled the cell with a forest full of leaves, branches, flowers and birds. When, at dawn, the girl and the reindeer were gone in one leap, I could still smell her on the walls. In the dusk, she left me her shadow tinged with the scent of honeysuckle. I saw long, straight candles burn around the iron bed. The wax as it melted spread over the ground like the first snowfall. The girl was still there, before my eyes, serious and quiet. I felt strangely unnerved by the shape of her breast highlighted by shadows that the moonlight threw through the bars. I could hear her breathe. It seemed I had only to reach out my hand to touch her, but each time I tried her image would elude me. And I wanted to rub myself against her belly, make the kind of love that doesn't exist in this world, inventing her body and her movements. This vision dissolved as quickly as it had formed. Later, I learned that these hallucinations were common among prisoners. In the depths of the abyss, tortured men know this peaceful apparition that visits them when life shrinks. And, however unexpected she may be, her shapes somehow seem intimate to us.

I wrote to Bako, but had trouble formulating the words. My writing was even less confident than my speech. I hardly knew how to read. It took me hours to compose a letter, crossing out useless words again and again. To write. In the beginning my efforts were stiff and laborious. The simplest sentences made the muscles in my arm knot together, but little by little I became more skilful. It was a huge comfort to pour out my litany of sorrows onto paper.

Bako replied in clumsy notes, but the more he wrote, the more I sensed a surprising maturity in him too. I imagined him, head slightly to one side, holding the paper in his left hand while his right childishly traced the generous words of friendship. There was so much naivety and kindness in his letters, which described his days in prison. Through them, we were holding hands, like brothers who love each other. I kept them very carefully in their envelopes, tied together with my old shoelaces. Sometimes I reread them, out loud. I loved the touching lines where he cried his impatience for us to see each other again and fretted about the passing of time. Now we shared a new bond: prison. In my cell, I'd often try to remember his face.

Gradually, time became a kind of test. I had to fight against suffering. I no longer counted the years. The days, endlessly repeated, were divided into seconds, unto infinity. I measured them by the patch of morning light and the frail flame of a candle. Indifferent, the sun rose each dawn, wherever, over cities, roads, cemeteries, while sometimes from the window grille a hand would reach out.

In the spring, when the days grew longer, something changed in us. There was pollen in the air, midges, bees, so many tiny things whirling around, totally free. We had the feeling that outside everything was moving and dancing. The air was softer. We began to believe in summer, even here. On top of the high walls, I noticed the perfectly balanced pigeons; I envied them. My main entertainment was a chestnut tree, it was always bursting with branches and leaves. I counted the seasons: autumn, winter, spring, summer again. In summer, what I loved most was dusk. When the weather was fine and sunny, clear and luminous, I thought of the people who'd soon be going home. I dreamed of the coolness of their beds in bright, airy bedrooms. Through the prism of the bars and wire mesh, you could see a corner of sky; it was so blue. Clouds of birds nested on the prison roof. Outside, kids my age were living the love stories I dreamed about, under a gold and azure sky. The girls of my fantasies danced on my nerves. The fabric of their shimmering dresses, the spectrum of colours, dazzled my eyes. I was filled with new virility. Desire was a painful spasm in the belly. My experience of women was very limited, just a street boy's escapades. I couldn't control the unsettling images that paraded through that dreamy state, when I couldn't tell if I was very happy or, on the contrary, very sad.

In the mornings, I'd wake up with dark rings under my eyes. I'd hardly got to bed before I was yanking at myself like a monkey. I took that loneliness to the limit and made the trembling last. Ejaculation was still an illusion of life.

I threw myself into reading, with a passion; it shortened the crushing hours of waiting. I read slowly, pondering every word. I grabbed anything that came to hand, indiscriminately. If books had become so necessary to my survival, the reason was very simple: to forget my body and my senses, not to satisfy some frenetic need to learn. Yet, little by little, this accidental literature widened my knowledge of the world more than anything I'd experienced up till then.

It was in the little library at Savigny that I discovered François Villon. His old French language made the stones breathe. It was more enjoyable reading it here than anywhere else on earth. Reading became my way of escaping from prison; but this new liberty set me apart and scared me. A thousand things I'd never considered became clear to me. Sometimes, at night, sitting in my cell reading, I would suddenly hear the echo of a faraway voice from the street, and wonder how it felt to be fifteen and free. Could you let your heart run free or get lost in futile daydreams? I stood up and looked out through the bars.

When we were let out for exercise, Doe-Eyes would always stare at me. It was no good dodging his gaze; when his grin rested on me, it would instantly turn to a scowl. We watched each other out of the corner of our eyes. He was still trying to pick a fight with me. I was trying to keep out of his way. No chance. Our unfinished business grew more venomous by the day. One afternoon in the yard, in a fury, he leaped out in front of me and the first thing he did was spit at my feet.

'Alone are we, with just that shirt on your back?' His mouth was taut with nerves. Noisy laughter all round.

'Yes,' I snarled back, 'but you look like you need someone else's.'

'Fuck, d'you hear what he said?'

'So you're playing tough now?' he went on, his face defiant. 'You're going to get your head kicked in.' He swaggered up to me.

'You're the one who's asking for it,' I said.

The crucial moment had arrived. How I fought would settle the peace for months and months. I had to triumph in this ordeal. If I failed or showed fear, I'd had it.

The others had formed a circle and watched. Taking up a position, I followed the movement of his arms and legs while he circled round me. To fight, I had to imagine I was one of the young thugs I'd seen on the street, imitate the way they moved and spoke. That's how I found my strength, under this tough shell.

'Take back what you said,' he said menacingly. 'Apologise.'

He clenched his fists till the veins looked ready to burst.

'No. You're the one fucking with me.'

Sensing the battle was near, the crowd of kids started to yell. Doe-Eyes came even closer. We still circled round each other, face to face, tossing out insults. He threw himself at me. I heard the crowd shift and shout. His right fist got me on the mouth. Each attack prompted screams of joy. I had to dodge the blows. As soon as he leaned forward to throw a punch, I ducked my head. If I didn't show I could cut it, I'd be a laughing stock; every day I'd have a new opponent on my hands. I had to prove I wasn't a coward and I could fight. He charged at me, armed with a long rusty nail, and I went up close, grappled with him, tried to force up my knee between his thighs to hit him where it hurts. It was my only chance. But he tripped me and I stumbled. I lost my balance, both of us rolled onto the ground, and suddenly something sharp plunged into my belly. I knew at once he'd stuck me in the stomach. I was flooded with fear. I thought I was going to die any second. I remember I put my hand to my stomach, looked at it and saw my bloody palm. I let out a moan. I stayed like that, my head bowed, for what seemed a short time, groaning steadily. The blood started spurting again.

A whistle blew. I heard the sound of running feet and voices. One of the warders grabbed Doe-Eyes, who struggled violently, foaming at the lips, wild-eyed. They finally got him under control and dragged him to the end of the yard, where he screamed for all to hear:

'These kids are worse than the fuckin' jungle bunnies!'

The doctor examined me and declared it wasn't serious, I'd be fine with the right treatment. At night, despite a dose of tranquillisers, searing pain gnawed at my belly. I was scared I'd get an infection. I was still exhausted in the morning. Neck bent over, eyes half closed, the doctor came. His 'nothing serious' conclusion reassured me. But I stayed in bed for several days, longer than expected; as soon as I tried to stand up, I came over all dizzy.

After which, I was cured.

Months and years had slowly melted away in blind, mute days. Now I listened to the almost forgotten sound inside me: my heart, which had stopped long ago, was beating again. Because my sentence was coming to an end, I was given a job in the library. As the day of my release approached, my agitation turned to panic. I talked to myself out loud to try to contain my turmoil. Sleep plunged me into nightmares and I'd wake up trembling and running with sweat.

One afternoon, I was summoned to the office of the governor of the borstal. The warder came to fetch me. I expected a rough ride; I wasn't disappointed. With a boss's simplicity, he invited me to sit down on the chair in front of the prison guard. I sat down. He looked me straight in the eye.

'So, Tarik Hadjaj, now you're nearing the end of your period of detention,' he said good-naturedly. 'I wanted to have a chat with you before you regain your freedom. I hope you'll stop being such a brainless young hot-head.'

He stopped himself, then added:

'But I doubt it. You see, I've been governor of this place since before you were born. Believe you me, I've seen plenty of boys like you pass through here.'

I pretended to listen in a silence that he seemed to find profoundly interesting. I nodded vaguely to the flow of his words. His tone was solemn, slow and pompous.

'What came over you, to end up here? God only knows, but I can't see any good in you. I can tell, and believe you me, I'm better than the next man at judging these things.'

His little eyes were hidden behind round spectacles

which he put down on his desk from time to time before slipping them back on his nose.

'Yes, I know you think I'm exaggerating the facts unduly' – he went on to list the names of all those who'd come through his office before me – 'and here I am with you today, as I was with them yesterday. Let me be frank, my boy. Think about it when you're outside, before it's too late and your final verdict comes around. It's my duty to warn you.'

I struggled to answer in a way that would make him see I'd try to be worthy of his concern. He frowned, his forehead creased, he clasped his hands and placed them flat on the table, like an old actor in a melodrama.

'Yes, Mr Governor, sir, thank you for all your good advice.'

He started in surprise.

'I'm deeply grateful to you because, you see, it had never occurred to me to ask so many questions about myself.'

His astonishment grew. I half turned and walked to the door.

'Hang on. Wait a minute.' He eyed me coldly. 'Don't forget I'm the one who decides who gets their sentence reduced. Remember, there is no such thing as an accident. If you find yourself back between four walls, it means there's something inside you that wants it that way. You should respect the memory of this institution and the warders who've welcomed you. You are free to go. I'm glad I've been able to have this little chat with you.'

Back in my cell, I couldn't help mulling over the governor's words. Already the dread of freedom had set in. Even my breathing was in suspense. The future suddenly loomed before me, as terrifying as the past. Outside, I'd have to face the world again. I'd never imagined I'd feel like this on the eve of my release. It was no good repeating to myself that tomorrow I'd be free, I couldn't get used to it. I was gripped by fear, unbelievably restless. I could barely sleep that night, and the wait was exhausting. What would I do with my life, outside? I wondered. I couldn't imagine what would become of me.

The modest sum I'd earned doing various library jobs wouldn't get me very far. My clothes were in a terrible state. I'd grown so much I couldn't get them on. In the morning, the youth worker brought other clothes, which I had to try on in front of him. I looked like a scarecrow in the new clothes. In the afternoon, I walked out of the cell like a mummy with its bandages unrolled. Along the corridor, some of my fellow inmates managed to shake my hand as I made my way to the door to the street. The big rusty iron gate with its creaking hinges slammed behind me. I looked left and right to see if by any chance someone was waiting for me, someone to love me or kill me. But three years on, no one was there. The dead man's family obviously didn't bear a grudge; whatever, they'd forgotten me too.

I put down my case, straightened up and lit a cigarette. I tasted the smoke that dilated my lungs. There was a soft autumn sun that day. Suddenly exposed to the light, my eyes were like open wounds. A pinkish glow shimmered above the rooftops. I stood still for a moment longer. The air was deliciously refreshing. Then I turned up my jacket collar and set off, scuttling along the wall like a rat. The wind chased the first dead leaves before my feet. I moved away under the trees, taking short steps. I kept walking, without the slightest idea of where I was going. My legs didn't follow any clear direction but just kept to the path I was on. And yet, inside me was an urge to go somewhere, say something to someone. Above all to sleep, curled up in an unmade bed, and rest my solitude on an unknown woman's body. As I went on my way, I tried to think of a place I could go. In my pocket I gripped the few hostel addresses the youth worker had given me. At the end of the road, I turned round one last time to look at the borstal walls. They looked even greyer than I remembered. The air was so pure I had to lean on a tree to stop myself fainting. Eventually I sat down on the terrace of a café and waited for nearly an hour for my heart to pick up its old beat.

Everything looked different. They'd changed the world. The colour of the sky, the leaves on the trees, the clothes, the cars, the sounds people made and the way they moved; I no longer recognised anything. Most of all the people, all these people who surged forwards in such numbers, in a dense crowd, these faces, voices, stares, they belonged to another universe. Wide-eyed, I looked at my reflection in a shop window and didn't recognise myself. It was someone else I was looking at. Prison had changed me too much. I was out, but the kid I'd been was still inside. You don't come back from there. I kept going. In the street I was always turning back on myself, not knowing which way to go, like a bird that's flown its cage and circles the sky, lost in the vast space.

I walked a long time. The looks people gave me were shaming. I decided my sorry outfit was to blame. Night had fallen now and stars glittered in the streets. I began to feel drowsy. I fell asleep in a doorway with my hands folded over my stomach to stop my heart from throbbing through my body. With the noises of the night all around me, the crackling, breaths and creaks, the yowling of gutter cats, the roar of lorries, unreal and faraway. Remember not to move, shout or call out, just close your lips tight so your fear won't show, shut your blind eyes and let yourself slowly drift to sleep. I was sixteen years old. All my life I'd remember the late summer light which bathed that autumn day.

To begin with, I visited all the addresses on the list the youth worker had given me. From halfway houses to hostels, night shelters to social security offices, it was five days here and three days there. The probation board had provided me with three hundred francs. But what could I do with that? A hotel room was at least eighty francs a night. The Verlan, the Ilot, the Alésia and Aurore hostels were overcrowded, the same as prison, inside and out. The addresses of the national employment agency and agencies for temporary work were posted in hostel corridors. The adverts required references and experience. I filled in a form anyway and handed it to the man.

'You don't even have the eleven plus?' he inquired with a sympathetic smile.

'No,' I replied. He shook his head in commiseration.

Day after day and month after month, however hard I tried to find work, I came back with nothing. Clusters of men stood waiting everywhere. The endless round of the hostels, daily life with no prospects for tomorrow, exhausted, weary of waiting for whatever it is that never comes. I wandered through an overcast, sticky Paris where anything could happen and anything did. My days slipped by like boats on the water, drifting with the current. I begged, like a sleepwalker, not knowing where I was going. Everywhere, lines of destitute people crammed the pavements. Wherever I went I'd see them, starving and useless, dependent on government agencies for the poor which organised handouts on fixed dates. Queues formed outside the entrances to municipal buildings. The unemployed, thrust onto the streets in their thousands, slowly paced the avenues, along with the homeless from the big cities. The young, as wizened as the old, wandered aimlessly.

In this ruined world, to live and keep going become heroic feats for the humblest among us. You fall, you slide slowly to the bottom. Every day, you make one gesture less. There are things inside you that simply die of their own accord. Little by little you lose yourself, forget yourself. You drink. The liquid flows and floods your chest. You raise the bottle to your lips with a trembling hand. Red Cross, Secours Catholique, Secours Populaire, the job centre. I'd long since got used to the idea of my own degradation. Sometimes, one of us would discreetly lift the lid of a rubbish bin. I'd been accepted by one of those gangs of young drunks with toothless grins.

The underground trains passed, making a great racket. We were there, about ten of us, sitting on the plastic chairs, looking miserable and shifty. Behind the glass windows, the passengers stared at us with blank eyes. At first, those looks are annoying, then you don't notice any more, you get used to it. We went begging on the platforms. One of our advantages was the pity we inspired. We made a few francs. We spoke without knowing what we said, our voices dull and indistinct, lost in a distant echo. I looked at the others like us on the platform opposite.

We would stagger down the streets. The slightest gust of wind would knock us off balance and we'd drop like dead leaves. What can you do in a world where you can't see anything any more? Keep standing? I've seen many broken men. I stepped over them indifferently. A crust of bread stuck out of a rubbish bin, I took it and forced myself to break it, first with my hands and then with my teeth, but it was stale and unbelievably hard. I hung about pretty much everywhere and fell in with other gangs of bums. No one bothered about me. One more, one less, so what? Winter had arrived. We walked along, beaten by the wind, our bodies wrapped in ripped clothes, seeing only clay-coloured faces, blue mouths and split lips over blackened teeth.

The whole structure of Notre-Dame shook as the bell-tower sent out its peals of bronze. I ran up. Just in time; a few minutes more and I'd miss the people coming out of mass. I could hear the hymns sung by the choir in full voice.

A few old beggars were already in place in the golden-brown shadow of the nave, waiting for the alms that would follow.

The choirboy was swinging the censer; smoke fled from the holes in the copper-plated crucible with each movement of his wrist.

Women in their Sunday best, wrapped in heavy coats, streamed out in a buzz of chatter, distributing a few small coins in fervent moments. Young ladies with delicate waists passed by, born to radiate beauty, gusts of perfume stirring the air. How could you not sense the virginal unease which floods that tiny space of naked flesh between lace and collar? I breathed in the blond locks that escaped in curls and rolled down swan-like necks until I was dizzy, my eyes caressing the downy softness of their skin. The clasp on one of their handbags snapped shut before my outstretched hand. That day, in His infinite mercy, God had forgotten me yet again.

I stood in the square, waiting for nothing. The tramps

spilled onto the street. They wandered around with feverish eyes, muttering into their silence.

Always the same faces: the eternal cohort of the poor. All these strangers, overwhelmed by a heart they didn't even suspect they had. They slumped on the ground, along the pavements, in a heap of rags, ageless. Secours Catholique, Salvation Army, the Emmaüs hostel in rue du Château-des-Rentiers, hairy and unwashed, we queued before the hot plates in a greenish canteen, holding out our cups and plates for a brief respite from the cold winter streets. That look of the beggar who's given the cold shoulder, the sunken hunch, the scruffy hair; we learned all that in those sad days. We progressed slowly across the room. In the back kitchen, near the old gas ovens, I admired the shelves piled with cheap white china, as cracked as our heads. Then, after eating our fill, we went up to the dormitories with their barred windows that were so high we couldn't see out of them.

What became of them, all those people I fetched up next to, sharing rest for a night or two along rows of rusting bedsteads with their clammy, piss-stained mattresses? At the end of the room was a plaster crucifix where Christ looked down at us with an infinitely sorrowful expression. By the light of a bare bulb that hung from a long thread, I'd pull off my old shoes and hang my worn jacket on a wire hanger. With staring eyes, I'd stretch out on the metal bed amid snores and coughing fits. I'd stuff my papers under the pillow. In those days I felt so distant from myself. I could hear the stunted echo of my voice, a sad, lost sound, and the more I wanted to approach it, the further away it went. Because the poor have nothing, not even words. Just cries that range from a wail to a bellow. We were closer to beasts than men. We walked the trail that fear leaves behind as hunters approach, but none of us, ever, could express the stammering pain inside, which is the very tremor of our existence.

A kind of ghost had slipped inside my skin and walked with my legs at night. One evening, roaming around aimlessly, I passed a bar, peered through the glass and noticed shadows at the end of the brightly lit room. I went in and ordered a beer. I was drinking, lost in thought, when a young man who'd been propping up the bar came over. He offered me a drink. We spent the whole night drinking, joking and arguing. Slumped over, soundlessly smoking the dog-ends in the ashtrays under pale lamplight, we downed a few more glasses, just to get to know each other better.

Malou had an enigmatic smile that illuminated his delicate, young face. He seemed to be smiling at something lost, over there at the end of the world. A hypnotic, distant look came into his hard, dark, piercing eyes. He had a straight nose with quivering nostrils and fleshy, mobile lips that he sometimes pursed nervously. All his movements were highly charged. When he lit a cigarette his face would tense into an awful grimace and he'd fling away the burnt matchstick as if it were a flaming firecracker. I lived with him for eight months in a seedy hotel on rue Montorgueil, a foul-smelling place with dirty, cold rooms. Cockroaches nested in the base of the beds. Malou got me a job in an illegal workshop for immigrants where he'd moonlight from time to time, working alongside some Tamils for a pittance. We got a laughable sum for the work, just enough to pay for the room. In a stifling atmosphere, sitting at our machines we'd knock up trousers, dresses and suits. The others cut the buttonholes or sewed in zips.

Malou knew all the sweatshop networks of the clothing and leather industries around Sentier where floods of illegal workers came to swell the ranks of Yugoslavs, Turks and Pakistanis at the end of the assembly line. They cut out and fitted hundreds of skirts and dresses in record time. We all lived in fear of a police raid. By force of circumstance, many foreigners lived this way, dreading a deportation order. They were invisible and slipped surreptitiously through the streets. The Home Secretary boasted in high places that he'd been able to stem the flow of immigration in this time of recession.

We hung around the streets from one night to the next, living the nocturnal life of cats. At the first glimmer of dawn we'd return drunk through deserted streets where only a few tramps lay sleeping in the shelter of doorways. Every morning, on rue Tiquetonne, we'd pass an old couple, rag-and-bone dealers, who pushed a pram with wheels that creaked and jolted on the paving stones. Their hands, seamed with wrinkles, scrabbled vainly for treasures buried in the rubbish. This was how they progressed down every alley until the sun heralded early morning. The woman was very old and had no teeth, she was covered in warts and abscesses. She followed the man, dragging a dog on a leash that looked as knackered as she was. They carried a motley collection of objects randomly picked from the rubbish bins and went off grumbling. The old security guard at the hotel, a veteran from Shanghai who Malou called Mao, waved at us as we came in. Day and night he'd watch the comings and goings from behind his glass door. A ferocious Alsatian slept at his feet.

We doubled as street vendors in the rich tourist districts, doing an illicit trade in fake Vuitton handbags, imitation Lacoste shirts or copies of Rolex watches made in Barbès. I remember we even sold condoms, made in Taiwan, to the prostitutes down rue Saint-Denis, but the synthetic fibre didn't have the necessary elasticity and getting one on was no easy matter.

Someone where you come from might have dared to say: 'They are everything we are not.' Our intentions were sometimes good, but all the same we soon realised that good things were not for us. We fell back on what we could get: the worst. Occasionally Malou would disappear inexplicably and only come back with the daylight. He'd stop for a couple of days and then his nocturnal rambles would resume. There was a strange glow in his face that baffled me, a kind of demented gaiety. Wads of hundred-franc notes stuck out of his pockets. It gradually dawned on me where this money came from; maybe he'd wanted to keep his horrible adventures secret from me. Little packets of notes piled up on the kitchen table. Malou counted them one after the other. He only half divulged his secret, but his dissolute acts were written all over his face. I waited for the explanation of his sleazy nights to come from his own lips.

After that I found out about all the woods where Adonis and Psyche hung out. Among the shapes that slipped into the lowlife parade, I made a place for myself, hacking my way through, punching and kicking, at my own risk and peril.

Now there was nothing I didn't know about Malou's habits or the style of that teeming little world. One night, half drunk, I suddenly started hitting a man about the head with a stone I'd picked up, and I could never tell why. My third blow split his skull. I remember I took his wallet and a ring from his finger.

I no longer cared where I was at or where life was taking me. I didn't even feel shame any longer. My nature revealed itself in a clear-cut, sinister manner. I constantly debased myself, just allowing the night to consume me in its shadows. By launching myself headlong into this debauchery, perhaps I was trying to immerse myself in all the monstrous elements within my soul. I settled for a firm belief in all that was evil in the universe. There were times I felt such violent hatred towards everyone that it scared me. Sometimes our victims only just escaped with their lives. Then we'd disappear into the trees, impossible to catch. Of course, given the choice, we would prey on the weak, like hyenas. That's man's nature, always will be. We had to make them suffer what we had suffered for so many years. But there was no point hitting harder and harder; nothing could shatter what had already happened.

I can still hear the tone of Malou's voice in the woods when, his features sharpened by the tension of keeping watch, like a poacher sighting spoor in the moss, attentive to the slightest rustle in a tree, immersed in the smell of grass, stagnant water and mud, we waited for the phantoms of the night. Sometimes we caught the reflection of a star through the bowed branches. We crept forward in stealthy silence, holding our breath. Sometimes the hunt was long. The splatter of raindrops on sodden leaves was the only sound. Somewhere in the mist, a bird chirped carelessly.

Unsettling forms took shape, troubling apparitions emerged from railway station basements, car parks or bushes and criss-crossed each other in the shadows – spectres that crept and crawled down the leafy, rustling paths. Blood thudded at my temples, my ears buzzed, all I could hear was my own anxiety. Malou was amused by my angst. The full moon wreathed his face in blue light and gave his eyes the glint of precious stones. We walked through the wood, pushing aside the branches as we went, our feet sinking slightly in the moss.

Anything could have happened, we wouldn't have been surprised. I don't know what held us suspended just above the abyss. What were we seeking in those places of violence and pain? Ourselves, perhaps. Night had seeped beneath my skin and was spreading, unbeknownst to me. It had reached far inside me, swamping me, like the disgust we'd feel at daybreak, exchanging long wry stares. The smell of sex was even in our hair. As the early morning softly revealed the night's misadventures, I'd sit completely still and watch the sun rise. With time I learned to assume that glamour of terror which belongs to misty souls cloaked in black cloth and fever, the song of nightbirds.

Yes, I can still hear Malou's voice, joined by all those tense, compelling, ill-fated voices that rise from men's throats. And they echo in the soul, like a footstep in an empty cathedral.

The Brazilian transvestites' hair floated, at times hidden, at times visible, as troubling as spirits whose soul, body and sex are indivisible. We brushed against their silky dizziness. Some wore mock corsets of black lace that bared breasts yet held up stockings, so any voyeur who happened on the scene would surely have assumed this whole little world was one of the weaker sex. Every night they seemed to fall from the trees, soon to be confused with the other angels.

One of them, wearing a tailcoat and top hat, half naked, greeted cruising cars with an insolent bow and laughter cascading through the trees. The air was heavy with the scent of lilacs and the smell of bodies. More peals of laughter, which echoed on the other side of the path. But the fresh roses in their hair faded as the breaking of dawn gave way to beards and wrecked faces in the morning light. The grey pavements were strewn with wilted petals. Dishevelled and exhausted, we'd go home. With haggard eyes, sitting right on the edge of the bed, I'd pull off my shoes. Not bothering to undress, mind racing and nerves jangling, I'd flop down on the mattress and sink into the welcoming darkness. Sometimes, after our adventures, we'd go crazy and run after pretty girls in nightclubs where, over supper, under the soft lights, we'd count the night's takings.

Malou's nocturnal hunting caused him no shame or resentment; his skin bore traces of voracious lips and groping fingers. I almost envied him his cruel eyes: clear and cutting, devoid of false pity. I could never partake of those embraces myself; I had no urges of that kind. During our escapades, I realised that, even from a negative point of view, a rogue had a certain prestige in the eyes of classy, elegant people; a desirable yet uneasy fascination. How many times did I hide in the depths of the woods, waiting for Malou? He'd reappear, looking oddly radiant, staring at his hands, not saying a word, seeing only the banknotes he crumpled between his fingers. One evening in Buttes-Chaumont park, the grey outline of a man whose face we could barely see made overtures to us in a suave, flirtatious voice. He was leaning against a tree, smoking.

'Hi there,' said Malou. 'Got a smoke?'

'Sure I have.' The man tilted his head towards us in a friendly manner and proffered a gold cigarette case. We stood for a moment as the match flared briefly, drawing on the cigarette that lit up the shadows. He stood facing us and spoke almost in a whisper. Malou smiled at him, with a casual, mocking air.

'How old are you?'

'Seventeen.'

He pulled two five-hundred franc notes from his wallet and offered them to Malou, who pinched them gently between thumb and index finger as he might the wing of a dead butterfly, then put them in his trouser pocket.

'Shall we go?' he said simply.

Their faces were suddenly so close I might have been

watching them seal their wedding vows, when Malou head-butted him on the nose, with a heavy, flat thud. The blood spattered his forehead.

'Give us the dosh,' he spat in a tone that brooked no reply. I wore on my finger a burnished copper ring with a small coiled snake on it. The shape of the ring was soon stamped on the cheekbone of the man, who stammered in terror. He'd covered his face with his arms to protect himself and implored our pity. Malou had him by the wrist now. He slapped his face with the back of his hand. The man crumpled. His eyes bulged, he sobbed and groaned and crawled on the ground. He tried to grab my trouser hem, but Malou crushed his fingers under his heels. His screams rose to the tree tops. But the age-old moon had heard too many others plead in just the same way. He could scream all he liked, no one was listening. It was just one more cry in that rumbling moan which fills the world and spills over the edge of time. Malou played with the man as a cat plays with a mouse – ferociously. With his jacket, shirt and trousers off, he was white as snow, thin and fragile. Then Malou took a tube of red lipstick out of his pocket and smeared it over his mouth, to signify his sexuality. Now he was going mad, he was strangling him. I pulled him off, yanking him backwards violently. So that the man couldn't call the police immediately, I took his clothes. As we fled I saw him picking up dead leaves to cover his naked body.

At those moments I felt detached from myself. Part of me joined in with this extreme violence, another me observed it. Those acts seemed as unreal as if I'd committed them in my dreams, and yet I'd heard the man scream, lying belly to the ground, like a lamb to the slaughter. A kind of dissociation developed between my actions, thoughts and sensations. I could rarely make a whole of them. I was hell-bent on my own destruction.

I often had the feeling that neither my actions nor my will depended on me, that my fate had been decided by that other me who stood behind me and made me act in his place. In Malou's sheer physical violence, he seemed to be trying to deny some intimate part of himself with all the energy of despair. He prowled those male domains as if to prove what he was not. In this cruel game of pretences I could read his profound solitude. Now I knew that in his brief encounters he could go as far as the sacrificial murder of his victims. Because he himself was torn between his overweening desire and the pitiful individual whose life he led, day in day out. That part of his being which he couldn't cherish and caress he battered, distancing himself from the true self he could have become. His blows were a kind of liberating gesture, a way of reaching out to others. His hatred increasingly spoke of his desire to resist the call of nameless voices, like a song from the deep. Bodies twist and mingle in that violent complicity. Heads, thighs, torsos attract and repel each other. I felt that in these strangers Malou was trying to kill something unfathomably deep in himself. It seemed to me it was his own desire he left there, laid out stiff on the ground. Maybe he enjoyed it, this prey served up by the night. I wondered how such a fine body could be possessed by such a terrible soul. His face looked like a mask of flesh that told its own story, with no words. I saw in it all the memory and sadness of his other face. I was horrified by what it showed. I heard the silence in what he said, his malice was like my own in every detail; he bore that share of grief that lives in every human attachment, because we do not only kill what we hate. I had to leave before I gave in to this vertiginous vice, in which I now knew Malou wallowed. I could accept all the abuse, but those sordid acts were nothing but other, even more monstrous solitudes.

'Listen, Malou, I've got to stop now, because if I carry on with these adventures, it'll just get madder and madder. And that I refuse.'

'Well, if you ask me, nothing is so shameful that it can't be washed off with soap and water,' Malou admitted. 'Anyhow, I don't owe you an explanation. But shall I tell you something? Your worries, your remorse, it's all crap. Because there's no difference between men and dogs, just a tingling between the balls and us lot, we call that love! You can tell me, can you, what the point is of giving things pretty names? Bugger all, that's what I say. One hot squirt, and that's it.'

Although we were as despicable as each other, there was nothing left to say. From one pit of despair to the next, life is a matter of how far you can keep going to the end of the night. But later, in the well of solitude, there's the sadness, the immense fatigue when you remember those days. For a long time my head shrilled with those screams, laden with all kinds of echoes. The night before I left, there was an uneasiness in the air, a sombre silence we couldn't fill. The angel of death passed over. At the door, Malou suddenly gave me a hug and wished me luck. His face was melancholy. I walked away. At the end of the street I turned around and saw him leaning out of the window. He gave me a little wave. I never saw him again.

Then, among the stream of passing faces, a new one arrived in my life. This face was not the sort to pass unnoticed. When I think back to that time, I seem to see his perpetually mobile, fleeting silhouette loom through the heavy winter fog on street corners.

Mario was the most extraordinary guy I'd ever met. Banknotes flew through his quick fingers. He had the appearance of a happy man, he had youth, looks and money, and imagined the world and the women in it had been created to respond to the extravagance of his desires. Once we'd become friends, he told me all about his tricks and cunning games, endlessly recounting the prodigious details of his commerce with the female sex.

He knew all the cities of Europe, he'd been all over, forcing open every door that led to the wealth which surrounded him all his life. In Berlin, he had narrowly escaped being murdered by a rival whose wife he'd run off with. In Rome, he'd fallen for the mistress of a high Church dignitary. She loved him so passionately she lavished her fortune on the affair, setting him up in the finest hotels in Italy. The spurned lover, against his holy principles, initially decided to avenge himself, before being seduced in turn, for Mario liked to say his rosary at any altar he chose, listening to the solemn Latin mass. He was fond of the hymns to the Virgin; I knew him to be quite as likely to follow them in fervent rapture as to forget them – for however pure the hymns, nothing rises to God more freely than a woman's sigh. Between the sheets' silky folds, although venerable stone or wood figures held real beauty for him, he preferred real human faces. Later, in a wood, the bloody corpses of this unlawful couple were discovered, their hearts riddled with bullets. A revolver lay at their feet. Their identities were kept secret for a few days while the inquiry got under way. Although innocent, Mario had to flee, and he squandered his beloved couple's money at gaming tables.

For years on end, his survival depended solely on his naked body and his agile hands. All the same, his follies seemed to me less craven than the rationale of law-abiding, sensible people. His body was all muscle. His chest shone with a luxurious crop of curly, golden hair. I was enormously impressed by his numerous conquests; his amorous exploits were all written down in a black notebook entitled 'The Pleasures of Love'. I can still see us sitting together at a bar, waiting for some rich American women to appear, or strolling the galleries of desolate window displays that link the two entrances of the Ritz. The waiter, who knew us, would sit us as near as he dared to our eventual conquests, without arousing suspicion. This proximity made it easier to strike up conversation, going on snatches of sentences we'd overhear. Sometimes we'd pick up partners from among those showy women with their wide, flowing trousers, who were followed by husbands in fedoras, just like the old Hollywood stars. We'd escort them to famous landmarks, amusement parks or the souvenir shops. We'd take their photo in front of the Eiffel Tower. In those days we had many ephemeral liaisons. It was the most prosperous time of my life. I wore a pin-striped beige suit with a waistcoat and a watch-chain. With a bit of money, I finally felt at ease. Everything seemed possible, simple and effortless, even my ardent lust for life. I thought I'd finally found the dream world I'd longed for since I was young, as if I'd been born for the society of the women Mario introduced me to.

I was stunned by his vast general knowledge, which far surpassed the usual cocktail party chit-chat. This was confirmed later by the style of his seductions. Nowhere was he out of place, in a museum, a concert hall or just in the street. He had a library full of books, which were his passion: history, poetry, novels, biographies. However surprising it may seem, he was as erudite as he was seductive. He told me about the life of Alexander the Great, whom he idolised and talked about as if he'd known him.

'Now, that man owned everything,' he'd say, 'and he rejected it all, even his own shadow at the edge of his tomb.'

I am this man's child, his eyes seemed to say, son of the god of plumes and swords. He dreamed constantly of the rich dowagers who lived in the old rococo palaces of the Belle Époque, who always travelled with their gigolos.

'Did you know the term gigolo comes from jig? In the last century it meant the young man who frequented the balls outside Paris. I bet you haven't even seen that film *Casque d'or*?'

And he'd pirouette before me with the grace of a dancer. He was a regular at the dances in boulevard des Italiens. In those rectangular rooms with their conspiratorial darkness, where the sound system would blare languorous love songs to the furthest corners of the walls draped in dark red velvet, he'd learned to calculate the value of the earrings and the brooch fastened on his partner's blouse with the sharp, cold eye of a dealer, whispering sweet nothings all the while. Sitting in black leather armchairs in the corner of the bar by the dance floor, some are still waiting, as stiff as wax mannequins. Occasionally, one of these well-dressed young men, whose job is to play the lover, will light an English cigarette with a solid gold lighter. In time Mario had gravitated to the grand hotels of the Champs-Elysées which were now his patch, but he'd made his first conquests in the old tea-dances of the boulevards.

'You'll see,' he confided, 'Paris is overflowing with lonely hearts.'

I didn't dare tell him women intimidated me. His only dream was, between the sheets, to negotiate a profitable marriage with one of those creatures who, in their haute couture gowns, trailed their boredom behind them. Their mansions, like palaces, were maintained in princely opulence. Wherever he went, Mario mysteriously drew women to him, like bees to the calyx of a flower. A delicate scent always wafted about him. Gradually, Mario introduced me to the scene, and showed me ways in which to make the most of my personal assets. But perhaps I was already cut out for this life, judging by the little inclination I felt for any other. Patiently, he taught me good manners.

'Anyone can master these kinds of behaviour, they're just comedies of manners and etiquette, a question of elegance and distinction. Villainy is very well suited to fine feelings and politeness. Don't make the mistake of asking for money, that's too cynical for them. Get them into the habit of paying restaurant bills and picking up bar tabs. You have to ease them into buying you presents, more and more expensive ones.'

In this realm, I followed his words to the letter. With ridiculous thoroughness, I adopted studied poses, practised giving my words the sheen of sophistication they'd require for other people. I was getting into my role, almost guessing my partners' responses. I played at being a virtuous, courteous, loyal lover, all the things that would please them and that I was not. Taking care to wrap my words in all the right formulas, I became a paragon of hypocrisy. As the years went on, like a good bourgeois son, I carefully cultivated the finesse proper to gallant young men attempting to ingratiate themselves with women of the world. The ones who bestowed their favours were careful not to fall for us. They looked on us with a lascivious eye, as they might when caressing a greyhound or a racehorse with a fine coat and supple spine. Tiny details would mark them out: a crêpe de chine blouse from Yves Saint Laurent, or a mink casually thrown over the shoulder.

'Look at all those pearl necklaces. It's an insult they adorn such old necks,' Mario would murmur to me.

They delighted in the way our bodies moved – us, the sons of poor men they knew nothing about. At the height of my powers, that thought sharpened my senses with a pain that was almost exquisite. All those years of loneliness would emerge from my loins, my thighs and arms, but my penis lay colder than a dead snake. We were so far from love. This was nothing, just hate with a hard-on. I came because it was my nature to do so. But this negation of self through love could only engender a negation of self-love.

The husbands weren't in the least insulted that their wives should seek in younger arms the pleasures they'd long since been unable to provide. The sound of time passing was already a distant murmur to them. One night, one of them, his chest bare and flabby, his testicles withered, sat on the bed and looked at me. There was a glint of enigmatic desire in his eyes. For we had even rubbed shoulders with ancestors, silent, invisible apparitions who crossed the centuries, passing from one room to the next down the long corridors in these places of rarefied beauty, like zombies surging from the depths of the ages. Between their legs, we embraced centuries. One could say it was necrophilia. Maybe we'd have had greater pleasure sleeping with corpses. I grew more lucid the more debauched I became. I realised I only derived pleasure from anticipating the very worst in things. By now I'd had experience of all the sickly inventions of vice; I preferred perversity to pleasure. I was like the rich man who lives just as he likes, protected by his privileges. With a bit of money, things changed, became simpler and easier. I was finally living by honest means, in the clear light of day. I thought of those days of hunger when I was reduced to turning out my pockets, in vain. Now I lived in a pretty little room in a three-star hotel near Neuilly bridge with a view of the Seine. I had only myself and my appearance to worry about. Sometimes, I just wanted to be like everyone else, to piss and defecate, with none of it mattering a damn – in a word, happy.

Everything's for sale, isn't it? Bread, sex, arms, God – one way or another.

At first, I was a lousy lover. I jerked about all over the place, like a poodle.

'Pleasure can be learned,' Mario told me. As the days went on I got used to his delicate education. He taught me the essential sexual rituals of initiation indispensable to my career; positions, powders and potions that enabled me to have more orgasms and better ones, essential oils and plant extracts to increase stamina and stimulate the nervous system. That was all that separated us from animals. The naked female bodies beside us grew more numerous. We pirouetted, dancing a libidinous waltz, indulging the basest pleasures, plunging into the dark world of vice and luxury. I didn't care what happened to me, my mind and my senses were swirling with delirious desire.

We lived off these serpentine embraces, but were we possessing or possessed? All these brief encounters left me gorged with money and disgust. I was weary of old flesh and lost youth. I remembered how we procured these ladies' good graces, insulting their opulent homes like the shameless gardener who dares sleep with the master's wife in his bed, savouring the fine linen and embroidered pillows. Under sheets that half covered my body, ageing hands studded with gold wedding rings caressed me in their peculiar way. I watched my erect penis at the tips of their fingers. I heard bracelets jangle in my ear with the flick of their wrists. Under all these rings, my cock shimmered in a shower of stars. I felt as if it was displayed in a jeweller's shop window, wrought in gold, a gilt penis mounted in a stark setting. You have to have experienced it, this grief which flows between a working boy's legs.

Long months, grey and quiet, passed in this way. We

played the attentive escort to high-society women with shrill voices. Some revelled in their merry widow status. At receptions, a flute of champagne in hand, weaving his way amongst them, Mario dazzled his audience. He cut a very fine figure. He'd stand up abruptly, revealing to his companion the stiffening object between his legs. In full view, he'd drag her into the next room. How many times did I see Mario taking three women at once, kissing one, caressing the breasts of another, nipping the third with his teeth, pinching this one, biting the other, as they fell back laughing.

It was clear he enjoyed displaying himself like this. The great fire in him made him a superb lover. His thick arms were fine sculptures in living bronze. Women yielded to his supple loins and congratulated him on his boundless energy. Their every whim was satisfied with no effort or fatigue. I heard him groan with pleasure. His partner would climax to see him come in a violent shudder. They wrestled late into the night. I was nothing in comparison; it was impossible to compete with him. He could enjoy and possess everything in an instant.

It was frequenting those women that made me realise I hadn't lived for myself but against other people, and that living that way had no meaning. Never had I felt so useless and pitiful. Thanks to them, I'd gained and lost so many things. I wasn't a fool; even the value I placed on their money was humiliating. I had an uneasy feeling in those rooms that oozed wealth and good taste, a kind of confused repugnance towards everything around me, which seemed worse than the dismal hovels of my childhood where I'd fall asleep in the fusty half-light.

Mario was a welcome visitor to receptions organised by procurers, in the salons of the rich homes he took me to; he knew them all. One evening, he thrust me into the arms of a doctor's wife. 'She's all yours,' he said. Sunk in the armchair I'd been shown to by a pretty maid, I felt very anxious.

'Madame asks if you can wait for a moment.'

I waited, reading and rereading the same page in a magazine, struggling to concentrate. I'd have fled if I hadn't been sure I'd be letting Mario down. Finally I heard footsteps in the salon. There she was, standing in the doorway in sombre mood, wearing a see-through dress.

'So sorry I'm late, Tarik. You don't mind me using your first name, I hope?' she said.

She went into the bedroom before me. A bottle sat in an ice bucket on the bedside table. We'd hardly sat down on the edge of the bed before she kissed me violently, full on the mouth. Her arm was round my waist. She nibbled my shoulder and rubbed herself against my leg. I felt her breath move over my stomach, pointlessly. She leaned forward and then back, and swayed her massive rump. Her eyelashes fluttered and she stared hard into my eyes.

'You can't be all that innocent? No kidding!'

She burst out laughing, shaking her mane of tawny hair. Without knowing it she was biting into my fatigue, thinking only to mock my weakness. A kind of hysteria took hold of her. She breathed deeply, her lips pursed and her nostrils flared. It was as if she was determined to infuriate me. At first I pretended to ignore her. She stood up, picked up a book and went over to the conservatory, which was humid and full of greenery, crammed with a jungle of pot plants, a greenhouse with countless lilies in flower. She stretched out on a rattan chair. She read for a moment, her neck arching over pages which she flipped nervously. Naked in the bed, I waited patiently for her to calm down. She'd hardly put out one cigarette before her feverish fingers lit another. The tension mounted; I didn't move. She let out furious sighs, aimed at me. Her face twitched and trembled. All I could hear was the ticking of the clock I kept staring at in an attempt to appear composed. I hadn't made a sound when she shrieked: 'And I don't want to hear a word out of you!'

As I'd expected, she stood up, marched to the window and pulled aside the curtains. Then she came straight at me. Calmly lifting her fine silky dress up over her bare legs, she slipped into bed. She was pulling on a long cigarette holder, making the sheet ripple with her other hand. Her breasts loomed beneath the curls of her hair. She turned to me, legs tucked under, and with the tips of her toes gave my limp cock a shake. She burst into diabolical laughter.

'Well, then,' she sighed, her voice sarcastic and scornful, 'I suppose we'll just have to be patient and wait for now. Sit yourself down here.' She patted the space beside her.

'You've got me all worked up. What a shame to be landed with a killjoy like you. I want to drink, and I'm not going to stop till I'm legless. Come on. Pour me a drink.' Her eyes were shining. 'I want more!' she shouted. She was drowning in champagne. 'Go on, go on!' She looked at me, glass in hand. I was tipsy from the glasses we'd already downed. 'Have another!' she screamed. I couldn't take any more. 'Drink out of my hand!' I drank. 'Drink, drink, I want you to get drunk before me.'

She guzzled greedily, opening her legs obscenely. The champagne had run down her throat and chest, giving her a golden sheen. She hung a leg lazily out of the bed. Outside, a storm was brewing.

'Fetch that towel,' she commanded.

'What towel?'

'The one by the chair.'

'This one?'

'Yes.'

'What do you want me to do with it?'

'Wipe the sweat off my back.'

I held out the towel.

'Do it for me,' she said.

'Do what?'

'Wipe the sweat off my back.'

She rolled onto her belly with a deep sigh, revealing her side. She was warm and damp. I began to rub.

'Do I smell good?'

'Yes, why?'

'I'm clean, I had a bath after lunch.'

Her body relaxed and she stretched out her arms in a cross. She wanted me to lick her the way animals lick their young, beginning with the feet, going all the way up the legs to the hollow of the belly. I grabbed her ankle in the palm of my hand. I pressed my mouth to the sole of her foot. I felt her shudder. She wanted to test my virility. I threw myself onto her. I felt a violent surge in my loins. I used anything that came to mind. I talked dirty loudly, slowly, and I savoured the coarseness that linked me to this pleasure. I defiled her, on my knees, behind her, taking her in the rear, sinking deep into her flesh, until drool came out of her mouth and I heard a groan that might have been pain if she hadn't leaped like a carp in a pond. My body appeased, I slowly pulled out of her, my penis flecked with brown. After quickly pulling on my clothes, I fled down the service staircase, stumbling on the steps.

I was like a stray dog, wary of being patted. I've never known what to do when someone loved me a little. I had to learn. It took a while; I had no talent for it.

It was through Lise's body that I discovered pure joy. I was completely overwhelmed. I'd never felt an emotion of this kind. I forced myself not to let any of my feelings show, for Lise had touched a sensitive place where I never allowed anyone, and I was afraid she'd have too great a power over me. I didn't feel worthy of her. First it was a communion of the body and senses, then gradually, of the mind. And yet I refused to think of it, this happiness we shared. Lise was the first woman in this world for whom I felt an attachment. It made me anxious and insecure.

I couldn't get over how beautiful she was. It's a fine thing to be able see someone's heart through their skin. Her breasts were heavy and beautiful like a kind of fruit in the hand. I was submerged in the warmth of her bosom. Her face at the moment of orgasm looked younger to me, in every feature, a little girl stretched out with her eyes closed and her hair undone. No face had seemed so close since I was born. In her pale green-blue eyes I saw a crack as if in glass, transparent and fragile. I only knew the physical particularities of women. Under their clothed form, I simply imagined the curve of the breasts and hips and thighs sheathed in stockings. So of course I was unsettled, hurt and shocked by the nakedness that Lise offered me. Some women possess a desirable body which enfolds a secret, a mystery my eyes had pretended to ignore for fear of a grief not suited to my sex. As to love, for a long time the feeling had for me been reduced just to its sexual expression. I couldn't see anything else in me that might inspire an emotional bond.

I ran from what I feared. Women in love have the art of ripping a man's pretences away from him, until they expose him in his extreme solitude. Lise saw youth as an almond tree in blossom. In winter, all she saw was that garden. The blood of pleasure meandered through the curves of her body like water from a spring. She felt the flowering of happiness and I felt true pleasure for the first time. To my surprise, I felt something loosen in my stomach, something that came from far away. On the first days, as I got dressed, all I could think was to run, run now for the life of me, for fear of being conquered. In the hidden depths of my heart, I knew she gave me pleasure. My body passed through hers. I loved everything about her, even her aristocratic melancholy. The way she moved was special, leisurely and gracious, as natural to her as breathing.

When we had supper in her room, the wine and champagne made us light-headed. So we'd turn out the light and go to sleep in the big blue bed. Lise's carelessness with money fascinated me. I'd regularly accompany her now to dress designers, jewellers and antiques dealers. I discovered another woman, too, a quixotic romantic who wrote poems with no thought of publishing them and who loved art for what it reveals about human beings. Money doesn't fulfil a life that has no purpose, no aspirations, she'd say. She taught me to like painters and exhibitions. When we went to a restaurant or theatre, we'd often hear a little murmur, a wave of dismissive remarks about me. Lise couldn't care less what people said. She'd simply turn her head.

It was in an English bar on the Champs-Elysées that I saw Lise for the first time. She was exactly the kind of woman I pursued: perfume, luxury, money. Sitting in a crushed velvet armchair, she looked ravishing, supremely elegant in her tailored silk. A diamond brooch flashed from the lapel of her jacket. I glanced furtively at her fine gold jewels and graceful sensuality. I don't know if beauty is an illusion, created by the eyes of the beholder, but beauty there was in the energy that radiated from that face, that brow, those eyes, that noble chin. I saw something I'd never seen before, the light of youth in the lines of her face, like a dissonant chord.

The waiter serving her gave me the nod. I'd become a regular there. We often did each other small favours.

My opening line was the corniest in the book; I went over and asked for a light. The pianist was tinkling away at the back of the room, a few customers were talking quietly. Calm, sitting up straight, legs crossed, she looked at me coolly. I was embarrassed by her proud eyes. Her easy manner was in harmony with her graceful gestures and regular features. There was nothing pretentious in this formality of hers. It made a change from those metallic voices with their mocking tones.

She spoke as if she'd known me for years. She smoked exquisitely.

'Are you married?'

'I was, for twenty years, but my husband died in a plane crash, en route from Mexico to New York. With our only child.'

Since then, she'd lived alone.

I felt suddenly guilty at the person I'd become. I didn't

dare look at her. I put a cigarette to my lips, trying to act natural. I was on the point of telling this woman all the things I'd never told anyone. But I had no idea what it was to trust someone; it was beyond me. She began to talk about everything and nothing, fast and feverishly. She seemed to have a lot to say, groping for the right words, constantly changing tack. Her voice rarely strayed from a distinct, seductive tone. She told me a great deal about her life, as if I'd always known her. I don't know why, but people often trust me enough to confide their most intimate secrets. I'd use them for my own ends when the time came. She told stories of her travels with her friend, an ambassador, a refined man she'd left in the end, tired of the glittering ceremonies and her official duties that constantly demanded wit and courtesy.

'Feigning intelligence is so tiring,' she said, laughing, 'especially if you want to be convincing.'

Since her husband's death, Lise had rejected all marriage proposals, whoever they were from.

We spent the rest of the day talking, and in the evening we walked along the banks of the Seine. Her sense of humour was funny and serious at the same time. At times we'd stop to sit on a bench and talk some more. Her voice was soft, clear and melodious. She underlined her words with her long, ethereal fingers.

'And what about you, what do you do?'

'I'm afraid there's not much to tell,' I answered.

'But how do you live?'

'The thing is, my parents give me quite a lot. I'm still not very independent in that respect.'

She wanted me to talk about my childhood. I talked, as if it was nothing special.

My lies became more and more elaborate. I created an entire mythical existence for myself. When she asked where I was born or when I went to college, she was surprised to see me blush with embarrassment. She noticed I was oddly reticent. She shifted her interest elsewhere.

There was no way I could explain to her what I'd been before I knew her. I couldn't understand what she saw in me. I felt she was wrong about me, but I said nothing. Lise was very discreet, but she must have suspected I was hiding something behind this young-man-of-good-family façade. How could I confess to her that I belonged to a world in which life and death are equally violent, yet at times equally sweet? I couldn't say when it was that we became really close. I'd abruptly change the subject at any attempt to discover my secrets. Her eyes would rest on me, frank and peaceful. She laughed again and took my arm.

'Tell me, Tarik, can't a woman be friendly with a young man without provoking a scandal?'

Her face was like a mirror. Looking at myself in it, my eyes became softer, the way they once were. Her tenderness spread over my features. Lise blessed me with every gesture she made. She could reach out and touch what was fragile and broken in a person, the brightest and most vulnerable part – all the innocence of the world, dead before I was born, and buried deep within. In that restaurant in boulevard Saint-Germain, crowded with the local and bohemian bourgeoisie, I studied her silhouette framed against the light. With a pretty shift of the shoulder, she hitched up the shawl that was slipping down her back. At nearly fifty, she still attracted men's attention.

'I'm so glad you invited me,' I told her at the end of the

meal. A little tipsy, we left. I slipped my arm round her waist in the warmth of the evening. I could feel the consent of her soft, yielding weight against me. But I felt strangely wretched as I walked beside her. Her shawl floated in the wind. I was thinking of what might happen if Lise learned the truth about me. I realised I was doomed to unhappiness in the midst of this joy. From the grey alleys of the suburbs to the cells of Savigny, my life pursued me.

In her hotel, in the large room festooned with luxurious curtains and drapes, Lise sat down on the edge of the bed, stubbed out her long cigarette in the ashtray, then, with the tips of her toes, eased off her shoes. I went over to her, restraining myself from speaking or even putting my hands on hers. I was moved by the beauty of her body alongside my own. Her neck in the hollow of my shoulder, her legs beneath my thighs, her arms under my chest, it was as if we were pushing back time. Under her lingerie, Lise hid the mists of childhood between her legs. Her scent and my breath mingled as one.

Much later, we shared a cigarette. Resting my head on her chest and closing my eyes, I drifted off as she ran her fingers through my hair. My gaze lost in the middle distance, I saw blue spirals rising through the air. Only when you make love can you really know how another person feels. Orgasm is the world's consolation, the only thing that lasts and transcends life, however bad things may be. At dawn, I stroked Lise's hand, which still lay in mine.

'You have to believe in love,' she told me, 'because it lasts longer than we do. Who can tell where things will end?' The sun rose over the Eiffel Tower. On the horizon, the sky was clear and vast. Her eyes shone as she combed her hair.

Lise had a passion for life. She loved to keep moving, she loved travel. She had to wake up every morning with her suitcase packed. I think travelling was a way of escaping from herself, through the distraction of encounters in new locations.

She showed me places that had been closed to me before. She had money enough to stay in grand hotels, and she loved the charm of old palaces lined with red carpets and high French windows. We went from one place to the next. Lise opened the door to this previously forbidden luxury. Now I set foot in the bourgeois world, watched it come to life before my eyes. In the midst of so much privilege, I was a favoured guest who stank of the gutter. In the evenings, I'd catch sight of a young black washer-up in the kitchens, next to a mountain of silver cutlery. I wandered along the grand corridors, ran my fingers over marble, slept in beds with curtains and canopies. But, more important than the luxury surrounding me, Lise helped me to discover the dreams buried in the depths of my poverty. They shone brighter than the gold of the rich and all the emeralds in the world.

With her, I realised that, even surrounded by all this finery, I'd never stop being myself or dragging the cortège of my past behind me. She would have liked to heal me; she did calm me, always bringing me back to gentle nights, to an unbroken sensuality. Gradually, through the blending of our bodies, we became as one, in the tenderness that unites two souls. I sometimes watched her sleeping. I knew the day would come when we would part. We never spoke of that time which slips through lovers' hands like sand. As for my past, only death could put an end to it.

I was overwhelmed by her kindness. How could she want to be with me? She loved me as I would have liked to have been loved in another life, perhaps.

There comes a time in life when your eyes can only bear light, Lise would say. 'Look at them, I abhor the airs and graces of rich people, and I despise the kowtowing of the poor. I'm blind to any kind of subservience, I have no time for it any more.'

I observed them, those men and woman who cried out 'Hello, darling!' to passing strangers, their voices full of false sophistication. For them the world would never change. They inherited their fathers' ideas and for the most part lived in property that belonged to their grandparents. Nothing remotely human seemed able to touch them; their skin was strangely armour-plated. But in the shadow of marble tombs, where the night would come to confound them, they'd be nothing but bones among their ancestors' bones.

Night descended over the bay. The beach was empty. Lise was asleep. Sometimes, as I looked at her body, I thought about her beauty, which time had perfected but which one day it would turn to dust. From the hotel balcony, I watched a lone fisherman on the horizon pulling in his net from clear pools left by the tide. The day's sun, worn out, expired in the waves.

I decided to go down to the casino. When I got there, the place was already full of people. All the summer tourists from the grand hotels were there. The evening was getting under way, elegant young ladies were climbing the stairs, it was as if the banisters lit up for them. The idle local bourgeoisie stood around chatting. An Arab prince came down from his perch; he intercepted my gaze, vainly seeking an ally. Solid and erect in his black smoking jacket, his hands resting lightly on the edge of a green baize table, a man shoved forward a pile of counters with every spin of the wheel.

It's a five, an eight, a ten, a seven . . . His gestures were elegantly nonchalant, he had the divinely slow pace of the professional. I'd spotted him a mile off. The circle of players seemed mesmerised, caught up in the heady swirl. The amount they'd already lost had to be substantial. In the succinct ritual and strong emotion of gaming tables, the man was clearly taking his losses in his stride. He was still betting. No visible tension betrayed his nerves. In all the commotion, I thought of destiny's ball, of the croupier who would one day release it. In the criss-cross of lines and figures, I could read the wild enigma of chance. Everyone chances his luck his own way. Gambling has always given me the biggest thrill: the rolling ball in its orbit, a shining star, the lucky numbers, the green baize, the contrasting red and black, the money lost and won, the giddy, superstitious fever that frazzles the gambler's brain.

Along the coastal roads, lined with villas and flowering gardens, between the promontories and bays, I spent the best year of my life. The sea was very beautiful at night. A light breeze caressed our faces. A rocky shoreline cut across the beach. We could hear the sea crashing on the breakers, from the other side of the bay. I hugged Lise; she rested her head on my shoulder. We stayed like that for a little while, staring at the waves. I'd never felt so at ease with anyone. The lights shone on the ochre and white villas. The clouds were pink. Our steps took us on across the old deserted town, by the palm trees, towards the jetty. Lise was as light as air, she defied gravity, floating like a dream. Her gestures were so vivid that her arms seemed like wings to me, ready to fly.

'I'll take you to Venice one day,' she said in a voice like a child's. She smiled and I squeezed her tighter. Your heart beats louder when you're happy. She was that part of me which would last for ever. Sometimes, opening my eyes wide, I would watch her. I was afraid she'd disappear. But there she was, very much alive. I didn't deserve her. When she took my head in her hands, I hardly dared raise my face to hers. But it's impossible to keep hiding your eyes from those you love.

After supper, we'd climb the whole length of the promenade, up into the hills, along the paths that snaked between the villas. The air was soft and warm, heavy with the smell of acacia and pine. On the horizon, the sun went out like a fag-end of gold and fire. On the open sea, near the cape, we could see the lighthouse. I pulled up Lise's white shawl around her neck. Then we left, heading for the town and the headlights, for all that shines and moves on the asphalt.

Finally we flew off to Rome, a city suited to nomadic natures like ours. We strolled around the maze of narrow streets as if they were corridors. The white washing hanging from the windows flapped in the wind. The terrace tables lined the edge of the pavements, so geometrically close that the cars brushed them as they drove by. On the tables stood empty glasses smeared with a mixture of Chantilly cream and red lipstick. The waiters, all in white, carried napkins draped over their left arms. They shuttled in and out, laden with trays and glasses of all colours.

In the evening the throng grew. The elderly, children, men, women and priests came out and fed the commotion. There were crowds in the streets, on the pavements and in the road. I looked around in wonder. I'd never seen so much movement, so much light and colour. The range of different voices mingled with the honking of car horns and the buzz of the Vespas that zigzagged between passing people and buses. Young women in stiletto heels strutted amid wolf whistles and barking dogs. The whole scene formed a complete orchestra, a simultaneous song, a single movement. Arms swinging, legs stretching, heads swivelling every which way, mouths drawing breath, eyes rolling. Everywhere teemed with life – town halls, graveyards, cinemas, hotels, beaches, prisons, restaurants, taxis, bus stops, cafés. It was a loud and garish city, with colourful crowds of people conversing in fits and starts. They spoke with their mouths, their hands and eyes; they shouted and laughed. Traffic jams turned into operas in the middle of the squares. Unforgettable harmonies poured from drivers, from one car door to another. The melodies of angels, with their ecstatic harps, flutes and trumpets, are nothing beside the fanfare of Italian horns; all true music lovers will tell you that. A few days later, we left for Venice. That autumn, the high tide, the *acqua alta*, gave the city a singular appearance. Water flooded St Mark's Square and the basilica. Standing on an improvised boardwalk we watched, astonished, open-mouthed, as a gondola floated silently under the archways.

The two bronze Mori that have struck the hour for over four centuries, the winged lion, the Virgin and child in gilded copper, all that splendour died for me next to the Bridge of Sighs. Suspended in baroque style over the the *rio di palazzo*, it linked the Doges' Palace with the prison.

'This is the bridge prisoners would walk over before they appeared in front of their judges,' Lise told me. It was the only moment when they could see the lagoon, from the high openwork windows, and sigh for the liberty they'd lost for ever. It was when we stood in the magnificent room of the Great Council where the fearsome Venetian high court judges would converse, with its mosaic ceiling above the law court and the great painting by Tintoretto, in the rectangle, in the midst of gods, angels, prophets, evangelists, and the portraits of Oriental emperors, that Bako's sad face suddenly appeared to me in a myriad of diamonds, emeralds, rubies and topazes. Ever since my release from Savigny, I'd never stopped thinking about him, how he'd feel when he was free, and what help he'd need, besides the money orders and letters I sent him. I counted the days that separated him from us. The following week, I was in such a foul mood that Lise packed our bags.

There's a certain kind of female nakedness that no man's eyes are fit to look at. What you see in it is everything that comes through the skin, what it reveals about her, that suddenly unsettles and moves us. When you think about it, if love has become impossible in this world, the reason is probably our inability ever to fathom the mystery of other people or ourselves. So few people are worthy of love, and I'd happened on one of them.

With Lise, my heart was at peace, but I was sadder than ever. I was afraid I'd lose my way in my endless lies. It was as if my shame was written in my eyes. I dared not talk about my feelings and doubts or even dream that someone could accept me as I was, simply and completely, and not judge me. How could I have had such naive expectations? I could live with my lies, but not when I looked at Lise; in the long run that would be unbearable. Although she still gave me money, and promised me even more, I kept on thinking of leaving. More and more she wanted to know about my life. It seemed I was condemned to lie for ever. In order to tell the truth, I'd have had to talk about myself, which would have been too painful. The whole truth and nothing but the truth is a terrible commitment, and intolerable to live with. Lying at least distracts you, from yourself and other people.

'You can't live being truthful, Lise, because what comes out into the open is the very worst of mankind: cruelty. We all pretend to ignore it. Yes, Lise, I lie just the same as I breathe, and I don't aspire to truth.'

'If that's your choice, you shouldn't be ashamed of it.'

I looked up at her and flushed, forcing a smile to keep a semblance of good humour.

'In the end, it's up to you.'

It stunned me to hear her say that with so much conviction. It made me extremely uneasy. Later I sensed that all the same she was very worried by my confession, and I tried in vain to wriggle out of it. Lise wanted to share her most intimate self with me, but she was thwarted in this because she couldn't get a handle on my personality and that was a shock to her. One day when we were discussing dignity, she had a violent reaction, whereas I wasn't really bothered. She was soft-hearted enough to imagine that, like her, I admired the nobility of sacrifice and purity, and all that these embody. All I cared about was saving my skin, nothing else. My heart wasn't the least bit sensitive to the bigger picture. The smoke was still rising from men's ruins. The dead would never have permitted the praise, the crosses and the flowers heaped on them by the living. Poor Lise: with all her illusions she'd come into my life too late. I couldn't reach myself any more. She believed in God, I only believed in dust. To me, the faces of pure people are just like masks to hide the world's flaws from others; as convenient as the mask of beauty. Whereas the mask of ugliness can never save appearances – not even its own. But Lise was naive. I had a knack of inspiring love or pity in innocent hearts. That was enough for me, I had no pride. Life had taught me to see the executioner behind everyone's eyes.

'If we didn't hope to be able to help another human being, life would have no meaning. You mustn't forget that people have given up their lives to save their fellow men,' she added.

'Well, they're just idiots, then,' I said. 'Man can crawl on all fours up his genealogical tree, and whoever he's descended from, he's still nothing more than the chimpanzee he started off as.'

Good sense deserted me. Gripped by a kind of hysteria, I confessed what my former life had been, and added that I'd committed all those acts freely and deliberately. She tried to interrupt me, sounding slightly irritated. But I pressed on with my story. I'd been caught in my own trap, reduced to spitting out my past, which I did. But how else can you tell those sad secrets others weren't meant to hear?

Lise listened to me, dumbfounded. Nothing could stop me now.

What hurt her the most was that I was shattering the noble idea she'd formed of me. I saw her eyes fixed on the floor in front of her, her face closed to me. She couldn't take it. I stood still, boiling with rage.

'It's easy for people like you to talk about dignity.'

She knew what I was getting at.

'Money isn't everything,' she answered.

'Yes, but it's better than nothing, you must admit.'

'Obviously you've no problem appreciating other people's money,' she flung at me, her blue eyes full of hate.

I slapped her smack in the mouth, so hard that her teeth sank into her lip and she started to bleed. We were silent for a moment.

'I don't like your violence or your cowardice,' she said simply. She wiped away the tears that were brimming on her lashes. She seemed to be waiting for me to reply. But I hung my head in silence, bearing the brunt of her icy reproaches.

Parting seemed inevitable.

'Well,' I said eventually. 'I guess there's nothing for me to do but go. You know everything now.'

'Do as you please,' she answered, not even looking up. We lay beside each other that night like strangers. She had been so deeply upset by what I'd said that the next day she wouldn't say a word.

My life was nothing but a series of departures, a headlong flight, beginning with the times I'd run away as a child all those years ago. I was constantly fleeing a nameless shadow on my trail.

I knew I'd be on the run again the next day, at dawn. That last evening, before I fell asleep, I thought of all the wonderful days we'd spent together, Lise and I, and of the times leading up to them. But all good things come to an end, and the moment had come.

I had to leave. Whatever we do, life brings us back to heel. I spent that night tossing and turning in the bed. I pushed back the sheet and got up. Lise was asleep, lying on her stomach. I put on my trousers and shirt. Sitting on the edge of the bed, I pulled on my socks and shoes. I paced the living room for a long time. Through the window, the light shone over the bay and the water slid over the gleaming beach like black oil. We'd come a long way together, Lise and I. She hated me for what I was, which was worthless. I couldn't keep giving her what she wanted from me, from someone I was not. The truth was, I was no good to her. I'd clung to her, trying to find myself, but I think I'd been lost for too long.

I set about packing my bags at once, stuffing all my clothes into a travel bag without even bothering to fold them. Through the window came the low roar of the sea. An unusual melancholy pervaded the room, there was some weird dislocation in the silence of the night, like a dream deep in a sleeping soul.

Ten times I tried to write a note, but I couldn't express what I felt. I gave up; it seemed too elaborate or too stiff. I didn't have a penny to my name, but I'd made my decision to leave.

Before I crossed the threshold, I opened Lise's handbag. I was well aware it was a lowdown act, but I did it, although my reasons were unfathomable. I took her wallet. Among the papers were photos of me. So that there'd be no trace, I ripped them up. As she slept, I took her ring with the precious stone. I'd always seen her wear it. I pulled it gently off her finger. Just why did I do that? I think it was so as to break with any kind of sentimentality. With that gesture, I attempted to free myself from her, or free her from me. I'm not sure any more. And anyway, what's the difference? Silently, on tiptoe, I left, offering this act by way of a dedication. I went noiselessly down the staircase and crossed the lobby. I left the way a person advances, blindfolded, towards their fate.

On the planks of the hotel terrace the tables and chairs stood empty and the parasols were folded away. I walked past the bay where we'd lingered in the evenings. The seabirds soared above the waves. Now I was well on my way, nearing the path by the villas on the edge of the beach. I went down the wide avenue under the trees, the one that led to the station. Nothing stirred yet in the streets. As I slipped through the drowsing town, I looked back at the palm trees outlined on the far side of the hotel. I could still make out the diving board above the swimming pool, the open-air restaurant and its white pergola with red pillars and the ivy that climbed up the wall.

At the end of the road I looked back one last time. I thought I saw Lise on the steps of the hotel. She was gazing at the sea, looking right and left. I could just distinguish her slight silhouette and her hair floating in the wind. Or maybe my eyes were playing tricks. I knew I'd never see her again. I ran across the dark streets, heading for the centre of town. I reached the station, damp with sweat, bought a ticket, pocketed the change, walked to the platform and entered the compartment of a train. I sat down in a corner and settled down for a long ride. A man came in, looked around, greeted me and sat down opposite. He asked me a question. I just stared at him, all I wanted was to be left alone. He coughed, stood up, picked up his red leather bag and suitcase and went off to find another seat.

When the train pulled away, tears blurred my eyes. Once again I was running away, with a pounding heart. I wondered if there was anywhere in the world I could live without shame or fear. Slumped down on the banquette, I closed my eyes and slept the whole way. The train had already stopped when I awoke. I lifted the blind and looked through the window. Gare de Lyon. I'd arrived in Paris on a cold autumn night and I dragged my bag along deserted pavements.

I remembered Lise's words: 'Tarik, looking at you is like looking at the wind blow.'

Winter was over. Spring came. I had a letter from Bako, saying he'd soon be out. His release date had been set for the middle of summer.

When he came of age, Bako had been transferred to an adult prison and his record went with him. In my letters, I related all my adventures. Well, it all had to be said, one day. I longed to write to him about the sad, choked-up life I'd been living. In his last letter, he told me the day and the time he'd be arriving in Paris. As the days passed my anguish deepened.

The train had just pulled into the station. I rushed down the platform towards him. He fell into my arms, suitcase in hand. Although I'd kept the image of his face in my mind all those years, I hardly recognised him. We stayed like that, quite still on the platform. Tears spilled from our eyes; silent embraces and private childhood dreams on our faces. I quickly turned round so no onlookers would see my emotion. Much later, I looked at Bako's face. He seemed a different colour. His skin and hair were ashen. A tooth was missing from his smile of old. Swept by the draughts from trains pulling into the station, rooted on the platform, we found it hard to look at each other. Being together after so many years was overwhelming. We stood there, side by side, smiling and embarrassed. In six years, he'd changed enormously, but his voice still had that metallic timbre and slight lisp. I felt uneasy, as if this Bako wasn't the same one I'd known.

'Bako, d'you remember—'

'No, Tarik, I don't want to remember anything. Let's not talk about the past, if you don't mind,' he said in a sad voice.

He'd grown, he was almost six foot tall. Thin and nervy, he was now an imposing figure. He had stubborn features, very broad shoulders and a thin moustache. His handsome face had aged prematurely, his eyes in particular had lost their brilliance, which came as a shock to me. Something had hardened in his dreamy look. That cocky charm was gone, his expression was serious and weary now. There was a deep scar from a wound on his forehead.

Overjoyed to see him again, as if we'd parted only yesterday and he'd arranged to meet me here at this station, I grabbed him by the arm and dragged him off towards the square. We sat down inside a café. I gestured to a waiter, ordered things to eat and drink. 'You'll see, Bako, everything will be fine now.' I was speaking for both of us. I didn't know what I was saying any more. There were tears in his eyes. He looked away. On the way to the hotel, we struck up a conversation about the weather, to avoid bringing up memories of names that no longer had faces. We never once spoke of Sikko or Luc.

I carried his suitcase. It felt wonderful to walk beside him, he was like a brother who'd returned from a long journey. He had to catch his breath with every step. The noisy street seemed not to affect him. As soon as we got to the hotel, he'd hardly put away his things before he was opening the bottle of champagne I'd put on ice to celebrate his return. He set about it methodically, trying hard to muffle the joyous explosion. He filled the two cheap tumblers I'd picked up, then automatically put the bottle down. He murmured: 'It's so long since I've had champagne,' lifted the glass to his lips and drank.

Throughout the first week, Bako spent his days by the

window. He looked out over the rooftops, through the city haze, at who knows what. He never even noticed the weather. This detachment frightened me. His long seclusion had made him quarrelsome. Then we started going out at night. We picked up girls and took them on the razzle in bars. We'd only get back around six or seven in the morning, completely wasted, in full song.

How many times did we go to brothels, to love the ladies of the night and of the day, just for a moment, frozen in the contrite attitude of dogs taking a dump.

We were living in a small room in a boarding house. It had a narrow iron bed and a camp bed. We heard fights in the street every night. Only foreigners who worked on building sites stayed there, four or five to a room. One night, through the window, we saw two men start a knife-fight as they left a bar. One of them fell to the ground, stabbed in the heart. For days afterwards, there was a trail of crimson dried to black along the gutter. We moved out. That scene brought back too many bad memories.

We'd given up trying to find a place for ourselves in the world. There was no point starting anything. Now I could decipher the traces of the slow, dark days in Bako's face. At night, we'd walk beneath the stars, looking harmless, so as not to arouse suspicion, on opposite pavements. The sleepy city appeared deserted and dead, the streets were empty and the shops were closed. Only the pink and purple of the neon signs glowed in the sky. Cats scavenged in overflowing rubbish bins. Sometimes they'd knock off the lids, sending them clattering down on the street in a great clang of metal. Frightened, they'd leap away and hide under the parked cars.

That particular night, we walked up the boulevard until we reached a big car park surrounded by high white walls and an iron gate. There was a sign saying 'Private property'. We scaled the wall and found ourselves in an alley full of rows of luxury Mercedes and Porsches. Bako slipped along the cars trying all the door handles. They were locked. I glanced around; everything was quiet. With my screwdriver I forced the half-open window of a Jaguar and got inside. Then I heard a furious voice yelling: 'They're there!

There! Hiding in that car.' We'd been seen. We heard the guard's whistle.

Now we saw shocked faces appear at the windows of the building, raising the alarm, shouting from the rooftops. Electric torches pointed at us. First I heard whispers, then the sound of running feet. My heart beat faster. I glanced over at Bako, because some of the men held iron bars and looked menacing as they came closer. They whispered words of caution to each other, like a murmur in the wind. Bako leaped over a wall; I followed suit. More men ran up as reinforcements, carrying whips.

Looking back, I saw the shadows of our pursuers weave between the cars. Circles of torchlight shone in their hands. A police siren wailed at the far end of the street.

After a headlong rush down a steep slope, we cut across a low wall I knew, then suddenly lost our bearings – all we could see were the white walls of houses, all the same. My feet thudded in my head, my legs jumped out of my body. The iron gate loomed up again and we went over it.

Bako stumbled as we turned a street corner and scraped his knee; for a few seconds he lay on the ground. 'You can't stop!' I screamed. He got up and carried on running, lurching as he went. Alleys, avenues, dead ends, boulevards, in between the cars, red lights, flickering neon, one leg in front of the other, one arm forward, one arm back, jerkily, elbow to elbow, in this never-ending flight we learned all there is to learn about human nature. Spots danced before my eyes. Blood pulsed through my arteries. We ran, dripping with sweat, our soaking shirts stuck to our skin. They strained to catch up with us. We skimmed over the ground without touching it. I was hoping they'd collapse from exhaustion but they kept coming on all sides. So we had to run and run. We could hear them yell, swear and whistle, madder than rabid dogs. It felt as if the whole city was bearing down on us. Women and children on balconies shouted encouragement to them. One after the other, with a tiny crack, bullets whined past like wasps above our heads, maybe two millimetres from our temples. Two shots deafened me. One round skimmed past my right shoulder. A bullet grazed me like a tiny bite.

We dived down a narrow street that looked like it had a way through. With each step I felt the fear that throbs from beast to man. The beast you slaughter and the man you kill. This chase had given them a taste for cross-country hunting. I felt their breath rise behind me like the barking of dogs ravenous for fresh meat. My head rang with the brass horns of the hunt; we were the stags. They couldn't catch us now, at last we were safe. We collapsed in exhaustion against a large double door, stitches in our sides, red-faced and breathless. We stayed there for a long time in silence, letting our hearts return to normal.

Under the sky of a dewy dawn, at the end of the street I noticed a vehicle's rotating orange light striping the façades of houses. It was still dark. Two drowsy black men were criss-crossing the main roads before the rush began for the buses and metro stations. They were pulling containers on wheels, disappearing behind a pile of sacks and a mountain of cardboard, then reappearing with stacks of crates and boxes on their backs. Rags lay on the gleaming pavement, peelings, greasy paper, tins, oil-stained cloths and a whole lot of slimy rubbish. The noise of the skip, the screech of brakes, the piston, the strident chaos of the grinder coming closer. Two men in green fed the machine with great armfuls of filth that they heaved rhythmically into its mouth, without a word. They crossed the street from one side to the other and then ran to catch up with the truck. The rubbish bins hoisted onto the back ledge were grabbed by the jaws at the back and emptied. Sitting on the edge of the pavement, waiting for our hearts to stop racing, we watched them pass by, jump onto the footboards and hang off the truck that disappeared round the bend. Slowly the sun rose over the city.

The furnished room we lived in after that had a single window overlooking a dismal courtyard wedged between two sides of a building. Our dirty clothes were strewn all over the room. It was just somewhere to sleep but it was turning into a dump.

Fania cleared it up. She picked up our scattered washing, took it to the launderette, then put it away in the old wardrobe. We got into the habit of shaking out the gaudy blanket and folding back the bed, as thorough as soldiers. Even with three people, the room seemed bigger now. Fania's arrival had changed the atmosphere; we felt a lot better. Separated from the outside world, we shared everything, huddled in the warm alcove where a chilly breeze blew in through the half-open shutters. Fania brought back a small tabby cat she'd found in an alley. She changed its milk every day, pouring it into a chipped saucer. The cat would graciously lower its face to the saucer, stretch out the tip of its red satin tongue and fill the room with the soft sound of lapping. Fania sometimes fell asleep with the light on. I'd turn it off when I got in to find her dozing, with the cat curled up against her naked breast.

When she moved in with us, Bako took charge of settling her in. He'd met her in a neighbourhood bar one night. Their eyes met and she smiled at him. They had a drink together. She had nowhere to sleep. The next day, she arrived with her stuff. We were already living on top of each other, but who cared? Sometimes she'd tell me about her grandfather, a knife grinder and chair caner. He lived in a caravan parked on a pavement somewhere. She knew all the gypsy clans, every family. The children, the brothers, the sisters, the ones who went pilfering in the department stores or the subterranean walkways in the metro, even the youngest ones, the look-outs, who distracted shopkeepers or begged in gangs on the streets. Their hands clutched at the jackets or skirts of passers-by, imploring their help, while their mothers wandered the wide boulevards in long flowery dresses. For a bit of change they'd read the future in your palm, with flashing eyes. Their heavy, flowing hair fell to their waists and their skin was coppery like Indians'. Sometimes they cast spells and invoked evil spirits on people who didn't pay up. They mainly worked in places where there were lots of people. Fania's life and that of these women overlapped in an infinite sadness. They went here and there, scattered to the winds, thrown away like a fistful of wild grass.

Bako spent his days dreaming. I didn't trust his dreams, they'd never done me any good. His eyes always seemed to be drifting off towards melancholy secrets. At night, we'd all go about our own business. We'd only come back at dawn. The entrance hall was almost dark. We had to feel our way, groping along the damp, cracked plaster wall before we found the light at the foot of the staircase. We'd be so exhausted we'd throw ourselves on the bed and fall into a deep sleep.

Every evening, Fania applies her lipstick to attract attention. On deserted pavements, the silhouettes of stragglers vanish into the emptiness of night. The shadows disappear. Everything seems quiet and slow, yet in the madmen's heads thunder flashes; the noise of the city vibrates, sparks fly. Impassive as a statue, she stands on street corners, waiting to be approached. She seems miles away, not even noticing the slowing cars. At her feet, her shadow shrinks like a skin she's shed. Leaning backwards slightly, she swings her handbag with her right hand. Her black shoes sag under her weight, the lining's worn out. Behind the shutters of their rooms, people sleep, doors and windows boarded up, prisoners of plaster and stone; the cement has penetrated their flesh. Fania is wearing a blue dress that leaves the shoulders bare. Her face looks pale, more fragile than a mask. Heavy with waiting, staring at the bend of the road, a little sleepy, hand on hip, she sometimes lets her gaze wander over the bare branches of the trees. The wind lifts swirling dead leaves at her feet. A graceful anxiety flits under her long, curved eyelashes, like the eyes of a startled doe that cranes its neck in the forest. She goes in and out of the public toilets, along the damp, stinking corridors, where the air vibrates dully in the glow of pale grey neon bars, permeated by the smell of shit, sweat and piss. She stands with her legs apart. The flush washes everything away like a fresh water spring, cleansing her of all her stains. With a lump in her throat, she lies down anywhere, on a street corner, up against a door or a tree, or on the ground like a dog; she just waits for them to finish. So many men, heavy and light, have laid all their weight on her frail body. In her pocket are the banknotes they leave her.

There was never a day when she didn't have these encounters. She wouldn't get home till the early morning, and sleep would overcome her as she stroked the cat. She'd make it lie in her bed, snuggle up to it and breathe into its neck. She'd sleep with her head on her arm. Sometimes she'd wake up, feeling the warmth of the little animal against her. She'd stroke it with a heavy hand, feeling the spine's soft vibration through its back as it purred.

Fania was very shy and wore boys' pyjamas when she went to bed. When I got back, late in the afternoon, I'd fling open the tiny window and a timid ray of light would shine into the room. Fania would pull the blanket over her eyes; she'd be vaguely sulky as she emerged from her sleep. Sitting on the edge of the mattress, elbows on her knees, scratching her tousled hair and rubbing her eyes, she'd say: 'What time is it?' Then she'd fumble for a cigarette, light it and take a deep drag. I'd boil up two big cups of tea on the small electric stove and hand one to her, with the sugar. She'd slowly wake up, on the edge of herself.

Later, we'd go and have supper in the restaurant on the corner. Bako would usually meet us there. Being together, we felt a bittersweet happiness. We'd live by night. During the day, the sunlight passed through our unseeing eyes. It was March, and with all that long waiting on the street in all weathers, Fania soon succumbed to a heavy dose of flu. A short, dry cough scraped at her throat. She stayed in bed for a few days. When I came back on tiptoe, the cat, rolled up in a ball, stared at me with its yellow eyes. I'd turn on the electric radiator. Fania sank back under the covers, holding a bit of sheet in her hand. I noticed that she kept the blinds down on the days I didn't come back. She could live in constant half-light. I never spoke to her about the tracks on her arm, but I knew.

Sometimes she'd shoot up in her wrists. It was like a wasp sting, a burn that lasted several hours. One day when I suggested she stop, she snapped back: 'Look, other people going on about it is one thing, but not you, Tarik, you can't start giving me a hard time.' She spoke very slowly, to drive home the meaning of her words.

'Do I ask you why you don't do it? Do I?'

Scalding tears ran down her cheeks. I had no answer. She sat there facing me. She seemed so light a puff of wind would blow her away. 'Up till now we've lived together, all three of us, with no lies or anyone making a fuss. So we're not starting now. You know where I spend all my nights. You think I could go there even once without it?' She cried for a long time, in desperation. It wasn't much, you could hardly hear it, just a sound, a plaintive sigh. All the silent grief of the little people was in that voice, it echoed for a long time. Each of us tried their best to find a reason to go on; to try to pass judgement on our shared circumstances would have been absurd. We'd been escaping from judges since we were kids.

Another night, I listened to her breathe. I heard her cry noiselessly, in little sobs. The nausea that came from the pit of her stomach pained me. Both hands knotted round her belly, I watched her rock herself from side to side so she wouldn't faint. She heard her own voice as if from the end of a long corridor, broken, distorted, unintelligible. The air weighed like a stone on her chest. Her limbs trembled with long shivers that made her teeth chatter. The pain came and went in her stomach in sickening waves. The beating her body took made her quiver and twitch. Sweat streamed from her brow to her neck and dripped all down her back. The sinuous, blue-tinged lines of her swollen veins interlaced under her white, transparent skin. I noticed how pale she was, how thin; her eyes became two holes that let in the sky. She called me over and told me she couldn't stand the pain of withdrawal and that she wanted to die. I held her hand. She begged me to find her something at least to calm her down. Which I did, seeing how much she was suffering.

Slowly, her health improved. Still, she had relapses. But there was no cure for this situation, and no reason to hope for a miracle from anywhere.

'You should see a doctor,' I told her again. She kept scratching herself. Not much to start with, but later, because she went at it again and again with her nails, her skin was covered in scabs. She writhed before our eyes, her body shaking with convulsions. Bako would get up to reassure her too, calm her and give her confidence so the dizziness wouldn't claim her.

He stayed up with her through so many nights.

One late afternoon, I found her in bed fully dressed. It didn't surprise me, she was often so tired she'd fall asleep like that. But that day her mouth was open and she didn't move at all. 'Fania, Fania,' I cried. She didn't respond, didn't even turn her head. I put out my hand to shake her, refusing to understand. 'Fania. Fania!' I kept on calling her name but it was no use.

She was stretched out on the old mattress, her eyes pale and staring, arms and legs rigid, wearing Bako's shirt, which was far too big for her frail body. I jumped on top of her and pulled out the syringe that was still stuck in her veins and threw it across the room. I slipped my hand under her shirt where her heart was, to try a heart massage, and felt her heartbeat softly return. She opened her eyes and her eyelashes fluttered in the air. Her mouth gaped and she gasped for oxygen. She shifted slightly and groaned. I took her in my arms and shook her again. She looked up at me, wild-eyed, looked down, moved her lips, tried to speak but couldn't. She was panting on the bed, her breathing jerky, pupils dilated, forehead gleaming with sweat, her face twitching all over. I put my arms round her incredibly tiny waist. Through the shirt I could feel the hard ridge of her spine. She didn't weigh a thing. She floated in my arms. Without the contact of her hair against my cheek, it would have been a little like lifting the wind.

I laid her down again in the middle of the bed. She shook like a leaf. I took the blanket and put it over her; still she shivered. Her feverish hands met mine. I hugged her tighter and called her name. I stroked her, teased out the locks of hair on her forehead which were tangled with sweat. She burrowed against me; I leaned my head on hers. Her gaze flickered away from me. I tried again to massage her heart. She opened her eyes and gave the ghost of a smile, but her face was darkening, like a burst of light that instantly goes out. She went off again to the other side of words. The time left between her and life was shrinking by the second.

Deep in her eyes, I saw the city fall, the sky, the men on the pavement. She was lost to the call of night, sliding into the roots of the earth, in a still and frozen flight. Under her eyelids, life was fading. Her pupils contracted, she frowned. Her body folded like a straw. With a rush of blood, her fragile neck snapped. It fell back on her shoulder, too heavily. Fania lost consciousness. I felt a deep wave withdraw from her. Her throat rattled, her final heartbeat lingered a moment before subsiding. She floated in the air. Just to make sure, I took the pulse in her wrist and throat. But it was too late. She let herself go completely. Her soul rested in my hands. A chill that came up from her toes enveloped her calves, legs, thighs, stomach. An icy wind blew across her skin.

I stayed quiet in the silence. She was almost a stranger. I thought again of the first night I'd seen her. I'd never known how to tell her how close I felt to her, closer than I'd ever been to anyone. Her big lidless eyes, opened wide by invisible hands, stared into the shadows. I held her still in my arms for what seemed like a thousand years, as my muscles stiffened. Nothing could touch her now. All that remained of her was that backward glance as she lay on the iron bed. Night came from the depths of the world and covered her, redoubling the silence and solitude of the room. We were absolutely separate now, each of us absolutely alone. A kind of serenity spread over her face, in an infinite majesty. I closed her eyelids gently with the tip of my thumb. She looked as if she was sleeping peacefully. Now she resembled a child, her head crowned with tangled curls. Death had given her back her face.

A black-winged moth had flown through the window and was batting wildly against the lamp. Outside the dusk was rainy and grey. I heard the water run in the gutter. The open shutter slammed in the blustery wind. It was the kind of March weather that makes the world seem just one great, sad chaos. Rain drummed on the window. A moment later, all the sounds blurred except for the ticking of the tiny wheels of my watch in my pocket. The cat hesitantly put out its white paw to touch me. She miaowed and started to nibble me. After a while I stood up to pour her some milk.

The roses on the wallpaper trembled through my tears. I cried, for Fania, for me, for the world. From one grief to the next, everything starts all over again. The same sorrows rise repeatedly from the earth, give or take a few trivial variants. I'd promised myself I'd never shed another tear, but now I was shaken to the bone. My terrible boyhood panics resurfaced. I was lost, I was nobody's, nothing. I stayed sitting, my head bowed. I'd always had that fear of sudden endings. I could never cope with things that perish, faces that disappear, people you'll never see again and those you've already lost, somewhere in time, before you go and lose yourself, in memories that mingle with daylight ghosts dressed in shadows, among the dead who take something of you with them. I wanted her to live, Fania, a few more days or months or years, so we could tell each other the things we hadn't had the time to confide, our secrets. Life is sad. You can't save anyone.

I stayed like that in the dark, just watching over her, not thinking of sleep. The night's pale reflections diffused across the walls. All the people I knew who'd died appeared to me clearly, up close, and I retraced the course of their lives, which I'd so often so completely forgotten, as far back as their childhood dreams. I saw them. They stared at me with empty eyes. I cried again for all that melancholy, come from so far away, exactly like ours, so multifold you're ashamed that you only think of it when the dark of the night forces you to. Wherever we go, to the ends of the earth, over water or in the skies, death catches up with us. It's irreversible. The worst thing of all is the regret of having missed those who were, perhaps, waiting for us. We don't know where they come from, where they're going or who they are. They're so far away we can't even see their faces. Death digs a furrow in the earth, a strident call to fill the vertiginous silence. Then, on the other shore, we think of everything they've carried off into the shadows, the sadness that's even deeper than their tombs. And mourning grows heavier to bear from one loss to the next, unto infinity. It's as if one person's death drives us into the loneliness of all. And who knows what we will find of them, once the night is over? There's always something we regret not having said while there was still time, which we forget while people are alive; something we only remember when they're gone. It's hard to sleep at night for thinking about it. Suddenly it comes to us, all we couldn't say or do while they were there. When I'm alone with them, I'll have to tell them those secrets that no longer exist. I remember every one, as if they were each a little fragile, precious light. I looked in vain for a god to believe in, to pray to, but I knew no prayer, nor any god. I could call for help, scream verses in any language. No one hears the other. There's not a soul alive.

In this filthy room, death was stronger than prayers. By first light, its sinister smell was already leaking out of her through every orifice. As day broke, I heard the sound of cars being moved. Soon voices reached my ears. I found myself facing Bako. As I spoke to him, he looked down and stared at a corner of the window, his eyes blank, walled in silence. The room was a mess, clothes thrown over chairs, shoes everywhere. He coughed slightly and cleared his throat. He avoided looking at the body. Sweat beaded his brow and he fingered the collar of his shirt. He couldn't take it in at all, it was as if he hadn't heard me. Since he'd entered the room, he'd been somewhere else, very far away. Then he seemed to return and the dreamy expression disappeared from his face. He looked up, stared at Fania's body and shook his head. Then the tears came. It was as if he couldn't accept that life could stop like that. He crossed himself clumsily.

No longer in a daze, he went downstairs to call the police. They didn't hang about. They soon cleared the area and the yard too. I heard their footsteps in the corridor. The firemen were already busy with the body. I had to tell them the whole story. I answered their questions mechanically. Bako and I stood against the wall, stunned to the point of unconsciousness. I remember thinking: 'It's nothing, just a nightmare, I'll wake up in a minute and everything will be alive.'

A policeman asked me if she was my fiancée. I answered that she was just my friend. A few minutes later, the ambulance men arrived. There was no room to move. One of the firemen took off his helmet before Fania's body, as if to gather his thoughts. I saw his profile as he tilted his head. 'Poor kid,' he murmured. Now the sergeant was talking to me in a very low, almost confiding tone, as if to a friend or relative. He was a bald man, solidly built, with steel-rimmed glasses perched on the end of his nose. He only asked essential questions.

'Well, then, you will make yourself available to police for the inquiry. Have you examined the body, doctor? Good, right, what do you think?'

The doctor leaned over Fania silently and felt her hands. 'Had she been on drugs for a long time?' Two firemen lifted her off the bed and laid her on the stretcher.

'We can't get it through, guv.'

'Get what through?'

'Well . . . er . . . the body,' the voice replied.

The stretcher was too wide for the door. They took Fania gently in their arms and passed her through edgewise and upright. In the corridor they laid her out and took her down the old staircase. I heard the noise of their feet fade. The uniformed policemen brought up the rear. Through the window, I saw them at the far end of the paved yard. I watched them carry the stretcher to the edge of the pavement, lift it into the ambulance and set off.

I knew another part of our lives was dying. Yet I thought I'd exhausted all the fear that was in me, and all the grief. I couldn't go on. I wanted to close my eyes to the world, see nothing. It was inconceivable that life should be the infinite repetition of death. We looked at each other, Bako and I, not knowing what to do. That night, we slept in the room, utterly lost. The cat had curled up on Fania's clothes and observed me fondly. My fingers skimmed over the top of her skull and slid down her silky back. Her dark eyes didn't blink, but they narrowed slightly, in anticipation of the caress to come. I felt the light, almost imperceptible tremor of her body purring. She lifted her head to look at me. A feminine gesture.

The next morning, the police came back to see us in the course of their inquiry. They told us Fania was in the morgue.

The attendant, an old man, led the way. His grey hair had turned white right there, under the eyes of the dead. 'Follow me,' he said. A few people shuffled in the corridor. A woman in black sitting on a chair hid her face in a handkerchief. It was a real labyrinth. The place had a strange smell, of formalin and molluscs, oil and eggs, like a dirty tide. It was a journey from the outside world to the inner. A kind of obscure complicity seemed to prevail among these laid-out, wounded corpses. They were like statues, gnawed by earth which had altered their colouring and touched up their shapes, but their hollow eyes, filled with winter rains, spilled water that looked like tears.

All the anonymous people buried under a few shovelfuls of earth in the common grave lay there on a row of steel trolleys, in a long line. 'X' brought in, 'Y' buried; they die without a name. I could see yet more rooms at the end of the corridor, deep as caves. The smell made my head swim. It seeped right into my heart, the stench of rotting carcasses. The walls were steeped in it, like the rooms where the dead are dissected. We went through Emergencies. The railings in the lift were rusty and the iron floor slimy, coated in accumulated layers of blood and hastily scattered sawdust. And always that sweetish smell of viscera and warm blood, like the smell of animal guts drawn out all day long in abattoirs, bundles of freshly extracted steaming entrails. So many heavy, dirty doors with worn handles, so many trolleys stacked up, metal on metal, beneath the liquid light. We covered kilometres following that man. He jangled the bunch of keys in his hand. His head suddenly turned towards us and he murmured: 'Here we are.' He scanned the lockers built into the walls and kept pausing to compare the numbers with a list of names on the sheet in his hand. Eventually he stopped, raised his arm and opened a drawer. He bent over the body and slowly drew back the sheet. 'This is her, isn't it?' he asked gruffly.

And sure enough, there, in the cold shadow surrounded by an icy mist, lay the already mummified corpse: lips grey, face blue. The closed eyelids were tinged brown with black flecks. Rigid, petrified with the cold, Fania rested in a waxy plastic bag. For a second I thought she was going to wake up and come with us. I could only hear the wheeze of my own breathing and the shrill hum of the cold chamber generators where the corpses were frozen. Fania lay there, a number on the wall, a label on her toe. Her fingers were still clenched, turned in and purple, like children's who sleep with their fists screwed up.

'Their fingers are often like that,' said the morgue attendant. 'You know, the lines on the hands are first to go. Sometimes we have to break them in order to identify them.' Her head was tilted slightly to her right shoulder, her jaw was closed, her face a fleshless mask. She looked translucent. Nothing of her spirit remained. Bako's eyes were clouded with a mixture of shock and grief. In this room with its damp tiles and its dark green light from fluorescent tubes, we stood speechless, overwhelmed by the silence of the grave. I felt a vein throb in my forehead. Bako moved his lips as if trying to speak, but no sound emerged. Fania's face still bore a trace of that sad, soft smile, a smile that couldn't be erased, even in death. They'd cut off her luxuriant dark hair. Bako tried to straighten her tiny, contorted bare feet, but they'd gone hard as wood. The bones cracked in the cup of his palm. It was at that moment, through blurred eyes, that I saw Fania's body escape through the opening at the top of the wall, and her child's skull, a nest of lice, sparkle with golden dust in the light that carried it off. She flew far away, beyond everything, where no one could touch her. She passed, light as a gull, breasting the wind, wreathed in a halo of transparent light. Fania's soul was air, nothing but air. She floated outside time. Divine virgins, receive her meagre remains without veils or flowers or crowns. Black Madonna, in your infinite mercy, receive her soul, her death knows your own.

The attendant had stood to one side. As we left, he gave us a little bag with Fania's hair in it. Bako bought a bottle of eau de Cologne. Back at our place, he poured it over the hair. As the days went on, the idea of sleeping in that room where Fania had lived became unbearable. Her absence inhabited the space so intensely we couldn't get it out of our heads. When we forgot her in life we'd meet her in our dreams. I'd barely dropped off when I'd wake with a start. The memory of her neck, her knees, her shoulders kept appearing successively where she'd slept. Her body gradually took shape in the room and swirled in the shadows. In the end she was there completely.

Sometimes I felt a breeze sweep into the room. The window had opened noiselessly a few moments before. Suddenly I sensed Fania fluttering on the walls, sitting on the chair, her face sunk in shadow, staring at me earnestly. She was there, about to approach, a hair's breadth from really coming over. Every night she'd sit like that, facing me, looking me straight in the eye as if she wanted to tell me something, but it was nothing, nothing but the soul of the spirits who watch us but don't see us. I tried to grasp her luminous form but she eluded me. She would be walking on the other side of the road to me, she'd be climbing a hill. I tried in vain to call her, and would wake up in a sweat.

The cat was still there. We made her life secure and comfortable. She got fatter by the day, her sides swelled. Bako would often talk to her under his breath. He made up stories for her. He told her he'd never lose her, she'd always have her saucer of milk, morning and night, she'd always sleep here, in this room, and nothing bad would ever happen to us, there was nothing to be afraid of in heaven or on earth. I thought with real nostalgia of the time I'd spent with Lise, two years before. Little things she used to say came back to me. It made the fact of living seem all the more derisory.

On a cold wistful winter evening, I found myself in the warm space of a room, as a fire burnt in the grate. The flames of my dreams cast dancing shadows on the walls. The memory of a girl over a fragile winter seemed like something miraculous in the air, of almost rarefied purity. A soft wind blew, like a hand ruffling hair. Again and again, all through the night, the same dream came back to me.

The girl's face was flushed with happiness, that bright pink which glows on innocent cheeks. She was walking in the street. I inhaled the scent of childhood on her hair. Like a light wine, I drank in the fresh dew that dripped from the branches of trees. Great trellises of sunshine filtered from the tops of mountains. The air was luminous, transparent. Bells pealed through the evening air. Paving stones were radiant with flowers, a dazzling, gold-tinged field shivered with forget-me-nots, an early spring raced with its nymphs from the mountains and plains on to the pavements. The street was bathed in reflections of red, white and pink fringed with gold, pollen clouds fluttered about. Passers-by, lighter than air, seemed to be free of the weight of their bodies. Life was a carnival, all colourful skirts, masks and blindfolds. Grandmothers with toothless smiles and long black shawls that fell over their thin shoulders blessed and anointed guttersnipes. Garlands hung from lamp-posts, little blue-ribboned girls chased their hoops. Glowing paper lanterns, multicoloured balls, jugglers, magicians, hoops, balloons, kites, even the sound of a fanfare in the distance; the band was approaching, the brass glinted in the sun, the majorettes marched at the head of the cortège. Romany violins were being played on the square, gypsies told the future in big crystal balls, a Bohemian traveller paraded a white bear and monkeys jumped up and down like demons. A rainbow illuminated the road and the land. A black man strummed a banjo atop the clouds, the wind carried his carousel tunes down the road. We kept walking. A humble crowd hailed us and threw bell-flowers along our path. Beggars in couples twirled to old waltzes.

Children capered round Fania and Bako, shouting: 'Long live the bride! Long live the groom!' Looking back over her shoulder, neck tilted to one side, so touching, so vulnerable, she gazed at the skies, her eyes following a line of clouds level with the trembling treetops, in the fine hazy light. Her head was crowned by a wreath of orange blossom. The hidden love of wretched human beings soared out of flop-houses, sleazy dens and cut-throat alleys. Murderers, thieves, blind men and whores threw grains of rice in the air. I heard the nuptial 'I do' at the wedding of dolls, as fragile as a bubble of soap, blown by a soft breath from the lips of a child. The newlyweds flew off over the roof of the world and came back down through the chimneys of houses, into people's sad souls.

Life resumed. Days passed, nights and mornings without her. Her ghost was ever-present, roving around the room. It knew us. We carried it with us, attached to our sides, her shadow between us two. Through how many nights, as I slept, did I hear her name spoken in my dreams? I only knew that this voice was a foreboding that hung over us. The cat was getting fatter before our eyes, as the four walls shrank. Sometimes I thought I saw Fania and the cat reunited. Neither Bako nor I knew where or when she'd been buried.

We could no longer live with the objects she'd seen and touched. That's when we had the idea of burning her hair, and her possessions with it. We put everything in a bag, not forgetting her glass rosary or the little cross that had adorned her neck. A pile of pins and hair languished in a corner of the room. We gathered it up, along with the cardboard box containing her other bits and pieces, which had been hurriedly packed up after her death. We wrapped them in the sheet she had slept in.

Then we took the bus to the end of the line, towards the rubbish dump. The journey was painful, neither of us uttered a word. We went to the far end of a building site in the middle of a field. Bako had trouble finding wood, there was hardly a twig to be seen. When he'd finally gathered the makings of a fire, we put Fania's belongings on top along with a bunch of roses we'd bought on the way from a flower stall. Bako sprinkled some petrol over it all and threw in a lighted match. He leaned over the smouldering flames, shielding them with his arms while I blew.

The clothes and heavily scented flowers caught fire, flaring up in the evening air, like a bonfire for Saint Genet. There was a nasty, acrid smell. The blaze hissed and slowly quivered. As the flames grew higher and the matter melted, I thought I saw a woman's body dancing in the light, glowing orange and pink, with blue-tinted ashes round the living form. Perhaps it was Fania's soul that breathed and swayed there. Her features were masked by smoke, like those of a kid behind a steamed-up windowpane, pressing half-close lips against it and leaving an imprint in one hot breath. I saw her face in the all-consuming fire.

Combustion was swift. The air was heavy with the smell

of roses and hair. I watched her flesh turn to glowing embers. We stood a few feet away from the transparent blaze. Bako was mesmerised by the flickering flames. Oh, if only we could bring Fania back to life, just by breathing on the hot, fiery embers. When everything had been burnt, nothing was left but ash, which we gathered and wrapped up in a handkerchief.

We decided to go to Saintes-Maries-de-la-Mer to scatter the ashes. We knew Fania had wanted her soul to rest there, among her people. A mate of Bako's, little Louis, a scrap merchant at La Courneuve, lent us a white Citroën DS. It was spotless, thanks to those boring weekends when no one knows what to do. We had the oil, water and tyre pressure checked and the windscreen washed. The car sparkled. We drove off, hearts palpitating.

At that time of day, the flow of traffic on the motorway was light in spite of the weekend exodus; just a few family cars or the occasional lorry. Turning the steering wheel slightly to right or left, minimal pressure on the accelerator, a glance in the rear-view mirror, and the city receded from view. We were driving quite fast now. On the motorway slip road a young couple, two hitchhikers, stuck out their thumbs, inhaling the dry, clear, early morning air, waiting for God knows what, as a pink sun rose over the hills behind them.

The car, used to rough handling over millions of kilometres through city streets, sudden braking and crunching of gears, flew down the tarmac that opened up ahead. The lines of the countryside passed by, trees, telegraph poles, hillocks, filling stations, the road unrolled beneath the tyres like a long black carpet. We were doing 130 km per hour. My eyes were trained on the horizon, where my thoughts appeared. The sun's shadows shortened. Arms resting on the steering wheel, foot on the accelerator, eyes on the dashboard, in the raucous growl of the engine and the exhaust pipe, I enjoyed the feeling that I could drive like this unto infinity. Bako's shirt billowed in the warm air sweeping in through the open windows.

The tyres screeched on the bends. We left the countryside behind us in a trail of light. It was muggy now. My hands were sweaty on the steering wheel. I could feel my heartbeat in my palms, I wiped them on my trousers, one after the other. The sun was at its zenith. It was burning. A heavy smell of rubber rose from the tyres on the tarmac. On the back seat, the cat mewed as the heat invaded her fur. Bako had put the ashes, wrapped in the white handkerchief, at the back of the glove box. The engine droned on. I drove smoothly. The dials on the dashboard were bathed in sunlight. Midges got flattened on the windscreen with a splat. We only stopped once, at a petrol station, to fill up and have a coffee.

The sky was bare, not a cloud in sight. The sun glittered on the car bonnet. The cat dozed, nodding her head. Bako too closed his eyes and drifted into a half-sleep, emerging to listen to the news on the radio. Then he fell asleep again. The car sped over the asphalt. Light slanted down from the sky and bounced off the road. On the embankments, the undergrowth, whitened earth and pebbles danced as the countryside flew by. The drive from Paris had been easy, we'd respected the speed limits. The heat beat down on the metal doors and on the roof. Our tangled hair blew about in the wind.

It was late afternoon when I reached the hill. My eyes were glued to the road, I put my foot down on the accelerator. Halfway up, a juggernaut was toiling, pumping out a stench of diesel. I drove behind it for a long time. At the curve of a bend, I tried to overtake. There was no time to think. A blue lorry suddenly appeared, heading straight for us, engine roaring. My foot slammed down on the brake pedal. My hands gripped the wheel. There was a piercing noise of sheet metal ripping. Then came the collision. I turned hard to the left, to the right, but the car was on its side, it was impossible to get back on course. The steering wheel spun round in a void. We were thrown all over the place. First we went into a slide, then skidded out of control. The engine started to vibrate and the bodywork burst in the air.

I hadn't heard the sound of the lorry's engine until it appeared at the curve of the bend in a shriek of brakes, a screech of tyres and whistling sounds, punctuated by the honking of horns. It slammed head-on into the car, which veered left then right, crashing onto its roof and rolling over, then smashed to pieces: shedding doors, steering wheel, bonnet. Everything flew off: wings, headlights, wheels. It was like a mechanical ballet in a haze of black smoke. The windscreen splintered into smithereens, littering the asphalt with shards of glass and blood. They reflected each other in demented flashes of light. The back wheels had been lifted off the ground.

My head smashed into the steering wheel in a long squeal of brakes, at the very moment I saw a car wheel roll straight towards the ravine. It preceded us in a perfect trajectory from the bonnet. Massive pain clutched my skull. From very far away, I heard a crunch of metal. Blood ran scarlet from my head, in a silent, regular flow like water from a tap, all down my arms to the tips of my fingers. For a very long time there was just silence. Over my hair came the muffled throb of a powerful engine and the sound of a wheel spinning. I felt a gust that made me swerve this way and that. For a fraction of a second, faces floated before my eyes, they screamed then laughed. My mouth filled with thick, bitter-tasting blood. The gust spun me round and round. The car was now just a whirling object, tossed and buffeted in the middle of the road.

Inside the car, life was draining away. From his body strapped upright in his seatbelt, Bako's head flopped back on the black leather seat. His seated torso still jerked spasmodically. I screamed with horror. The lorry's front wheels had come through the windscreen on the right, level with Bako's solar plexus. Its bumper had hit him on the side of the head. His eyes, rolled up to the sky, had popped out of their sockets. There wasn't even any blood yet. His face was still lit up by the glare of the explosion.

The force of the collision with the lorry had wrenched him round in his seat. I could only see his profile. Then the blood began to spurt abundantly. It streamed through the doors of the smoking car. Death had been instantaneous. He was carried off in his sleep, in one never-ending groan, his mouth flooded with reddish liquid. A jet of blood splattered my elbows and hands. My legs were crushed. The rear window frame had crumpled, like folds of material, over the cat. She struggled briefly. The miaow she attempted was less than a whisper of sound. A nasty smell came from her squashed sides. She was just a little bundle of bones. In my eyes almost all was black now. Yet when I least expected it, I started to see again.

In a dizzy swirl, but immensely serene, my wandering childhood came back with extraordinary clarity. But I couldn't see it with my eyes, it all flowed through the nape of my neck. I suddenly remembered ancient, distant things. I was aware of everything. The clearly delineated black stain at my feet was slowly dragging all the weight from my body, which collapsed towards my shadow. I could hear my heart beating far away in my temples, in my neck, in the palms of my hands, in my arteries. Death scurried like a rat in my veins. The lorry lay in a ditch, two wheels in the meadow, the other two on the road. In the middle of the tarmac, the black tyre marks were still visible. The engine spluttered and gasped.

The car had been catapulted in a shower of sparks and then hit the safety rail. The squeal in the midst of silence was deafening. The DS uprooted a cement balustrade and plunged into the ravine. It dropped like a stone to the bottom of a well after a vertiginous fall: a deluge of iron, bolts, pistons, gearbox flew through the air. Below, the steel carapace exploded in a ball of fire. All that was left of the white car was a coal-black reflection. Flames rose in straight lines, the light smoke cleared under an empty sky. It might have been a brief blaze of dry wood and weeds.

Hordes of wide-eyed gawpers arrived in swarms, slamming car doors. Their mouths twisted in ugly grimaces, they flocked to the sheer cliff edge, calling out to each other. A voice shouted: 'Come over here, there's a better view.' They made a diabolical racket as they charged, dragging dogs on leashes and kids by the hand. They trampled each other, stood on tiptoe to see better. Bodies piled up, shouting, barking. More people arrived and parked at the side of the road, leaving their engines running. They came in waves and fanned out, bellowing, leaning over and straining to see into the void, gesturing wildly in the confusion. The clamour grew louder. They were a vociferous mob: possessed and dizzy with excitement. The driver of the juggernaut kept on repeating, 'Nutters. Got to be nutters to drive like that.'

Only one young girl, pale and serious, stood alone by the side of the road and shook her head. Little by little she was overcome with sadness, as though she could feel some profound wickedness rising from this crowd exuding a strong, after-lunch breath. People stepped round the puddle of oil in the middle of the road. The tarmac drank up the blood.

Innumerable faces, gestures, sensations crowded into the few seconds that separated the road from the precipice. The faces that had peopled my life were like those trees by the roadside, barely glimpsed before they blur into the past. I tried in vain to stop the icy shiver that ran through me. The din the onlookers were making reached me in waves like the sound of bells. As though life continued on the other side of the threshold. Then I felt my chest empty of air. Over and beyond the upturned sky, I heard my last breath. It sounded exactly like water draining away. I heard the convulsive rattle of my death. My fear was gone.

Through nose, ears, mouth and eyes, I could feel it leave. Life departed through my orifices. I saw it disappear over there, somewhere between the iron poles that loomed over the road. I exited time in a flash of light. I could see, once more, those generations and centuries which count for nothing now, other than in some unknown corner of heaven.

All that appeared to me in a synthesis of stars, as I watched my body float above my eyes, I don't know where to. I don't know anything any more, not even my name. I think in literary Arabic it meant 'the forgotten'

already the wind was covering the sea with a thin layer of ash . . .

OTHER BLACKAMBER TITLES

The Cardamom Club
Jon Stock

Something Black in the Lentil Soup
Reshma S. Ruia

Typhoon
The Holy Woman
Qaisra Shahraz

Ma
All That Blue
Gaston-Paul Effa

Paddy Indian
The Uncoupling
Cauvery Madhavan

Foreday Morning
Paul Dash

Ancestors
Paul Crooks

Nothing but the Truth
Mark Wray

Hidden Lights
Joan Blaney

What Goes Around
Sylvester Young

Brixton Rock
Alex Wheatle

One Bright Child
Patricia Cumper